The Secret of the Scarlet Hand

"Our new acquisition is very special," Susan Cald-well, the museum director, told Nancy and her friends. "It's a carving of the face of Lord Pacal, the ancient king of Palenque, one of the most prominent Mayan cities. The ancient Maya believed that the carving held the king's spirit. It was a sacred object."

"Can we see it?" Nancy asked, intrigued.

Susan led them to a room fitted with floor-to-ceiling shelves and a massive storage case. She unlocked one of the drawers and removed a well-worn cardboard gift box.

"Not the most attractive packaging in the world," Susan admitted with a smile, "but it serves the purpose." With a flourish, she swept off the lid. "Here he is—Lord Pacal!"

The girls crowded around in anticipation, eager to see the priceless carving.

But there was nothing to see. The box was empty.

Nancy Drew
Mystery Stories

Available from MINSTREL Books

124

NANCY DREW®

THE SECRET OF THE SCARLET HAND

CAROLYN KEENE

A MINSTREL® BOOK

PUBLISHED BY POCKET BOOKS

New York   London   Toronto   Sydney   Tokyo   Singapore

This book is a work of fiction. Names, characters, places and incidents are products of the author's imagination or are used fictitiously. Any resemblance to actual events or locales or persons, living or dead, is entirely coincidental.

A MINSTREL PAPERBACK *ORIGINAL*

A Minstrel Book published by
POCKET BOOKS, a division of Simon & Schuster Inc.
1230 Avenue of the Americas, New York, NY 10020

Copyright © 1995 by Simon & Schuster Inc.
Produced by Mega-Books, Inc.

ISBN: 0-671-87207-9

First Minstrel Books printing April 1995

10 9 8 7 6 5 4 3 2 1

NANCY DREW, NANCY DREW MYSTERY STORIES, A MINSTREL BOOK and colophon are registered trademarks of Simon & Schuster Inc.

Cover art by Aleta Jenks

Printed in the U.S.A.

Contents

Contents

THE SECRET OF
THE SCARLET HAND

1

The King's Carving

"So this is Beech Hill!" Nancy Drew exclaimed. She and her two friends stepped out of their rental car and stared in awe at the mansion in front of them. The elegant building was made of red brick and pale stone. The rolling grounds surrounding the house were a lush green.

"It's totally amazing," said George Fayne, Nancy's slim, dark-haired friend. "Welcome to lifestyles of the rich and famous."

"Are you sure it's okay to go in dressed like this?" George's cousin Bess Marvin asked. She nervously smoothed her blond hair and tucked her crewneck sweater into a pair of jeans.

All three girls were dressed casually. They had

1

arrived in Washington, D.C., from River Heights the night before with Nancy's father, Carson Drew. He had invited them along on his trip to a legal seminar in the nation's capital.

"I'm sure we're dressed fine," Nancy assured Bess. "Remember, it's a museum now, not someone's estate. And we're just visiting my dad's friend Susan Caldwell. She's the director here."

"What kind of museum is it?" Bess asked.

"Dad told me they exhibit pre-Columbian art," Nancy explained. "He says it's all stuff from South and Central America, dating from before Christopher Columbus landed there."

"You mean art from the Aztec and Inca civilizations?" George's eyes lit up. "I remember studying them in world history."

Nancy pulled open the mansion's heavy, polished oak door. The girls stepped into a grand, marble-floored lobby. Nancy gave her name to a guard sitting behind a large oak desk. "Mrs. Caldwell is expecting me," she added.

As the guard phoned in their arrival, the three friends gazed around the octagonal lobby. Long galleries stretched off it in different directions.

"This is so elegant!" Bess sighed as she took in the shining marble floors, gleaming wood doors, and burnished brass fixtures. "Whoever used to own this house must have been really rich."

Just then a petite, middle-aged woman entered

the lobby through a side door. She had short blond hair and was wearing a tailored silk suit. The woman held out her hand to Nancy. "You *have* to be Nancy Drew," she said with a friendly smile. "You look so much like your father."

Nancy returned her smile. "Except for my hair," she said, gesturing to her shoulder-length reddish blond hair. "Everyone says I get it from my mother's side of the family."

Nancy's mother had died when she was a young child. Since then her father had raised her, along with the help of their housekeeper, Hannah Gruen.

Nancy introduced Susan Caldwell to Bess and George. "Dad sends his regards," she added.

"I hope I'll see him while you're here," Susan Caldwell said. "He and my husband were close friends in law school, but we haven't seen Carson for a few years now."

"I'm sure you'll get together," Nancy said. "He has to be in meetings all day, but most of his evenings are free."

"Well, would you like to see Beech Hill?" Susan asked. "It's an extraordinary place. Let me give you a tour."

Mrs. Caldwell led Nancy and her friends through a door into a high-ceilinged gallery. It was like entering another world. The gallery's free-standing glass cases and wall-mounted displays were filled with beautiful objects—bowls, medallions, small statues, ornaments—some made of gold, others of stone. Nancy was mesmerized by the objects' colors and textures.

"Beech Hill was originally the home of Samuel and Lavinia Cartwright," Susan Caldwell explained. "They bought the house and land in the 1930s and named it Beech Hill for the old copper beech tree in the main garden."

She continued talking as the girls admired the objects in the room. "When Samuel Cartwright was sent as the American ambassador to Mexico, he got interested in the native Indians who lived there before the Spanish arrived—the Olmec, Maya, and Aztec peoples. He started to collect pre-Columbian art, although other art collectors at the time thought he was crazy."

"Why?" Nancy asked. Looking at the beautiful objects in the gallery, it was hard to imagine anyone not being interested in them.

"They thought these were works by primitive, uneducated people—not art at all," Susan answered. "They thought it wasn't worth buying."

"It's a pity it didn't stay that way," a voice with a soft Latino accent spoke up behind them. Nancy turned and found herself facing a dark-haired young man with intense eyes.

"People like the Cartwrights stole my country's art," he said bitterly. "They locked it away so only rich Americans could see it."

"Beech Hill is open to the public," Susan pro-

4

tested. "Anyone can come here—you know that, Alejandro."

"It's not that simple." The young man scowled. "Is the art of *your* country thousands of miles away where your people can never see it?"

"Alejandro?" a brisk voice called from the next gallery. A gray-haired older man entered, his thick black spectacles magnifying the concerned look in his eyes.

"Hello, Henrik," Susan said. "Alejandro and I are having our usual discussion."

The director was obviously trying to play down Alejandro's anger. But Nancy could tell from Susan's expression that the young man's accusations bothered her.

The man called Henrik laid a friendly hand on Alejandro's shoulder. "My friend, you need to be more diplomatic." Nancy noticed that he spoke with an accent, too. She guessed he was German or Dutch. "After all, you are a diplomat," Henrik added with a smile. But his smile went unreturned. Instead Alejandro just glowered.

"I'm afraid I'm forgetting my manners," Mrs. Caldwell said, changing the subject. "Nancy Drew, George Fayne, and Bess Marvin, this is Henrik van der Hune, our curator. And this young fellow is Alejandro del Rio, a cultural attaché with the Mexican consulate."

The girls shook hands with van der Hune and del Rio as Susan explained how she knew Nancy and her friends and why they were at Beech Hill. Nancy couldn't help noticing that Alejandro del Rio refused to meet anyone's eyes.

"Alejandro is here to discuss the details of the Mexican consulate's exhibition next month," van der Hune told Susan. "We've been going over some of the objects we will be loaning them."

Del Rio turned to Susan. "Isn't the new carving you've acquired on exhibit yet?"

Susan paused before she replied. "No, the display case still isn't ready."

Del Rio sighed. "I've been waiting to see it. You know why," he added.

"Alejandro," Susan retorted sharply, "that piece came into this country years ago— well before the U.S. made it illegal to import Mexican antiquities. Isn't it better for it to be displayed here instead of being hidden away in someone's private collection, as it used to be?"

"The best situation would be to return it to my country," del Rio shot back.

"Alejandro, I hear what you say," van der Hune put in. "I somewhat agree with you, I must admit. It was wrong for American collectors to take the art of your country away."

"Honestly, Henrik, what's done is done." Susan frowned at the museum's curator. "Are we supposed to return everything now?"

"You could start with the carving you just bought," del Rio told her.

Before Susan could reply, van der Hune took del Rio by the elbow. "Come, Alejandro, we still have work to do," he said smoothly. "Good morning, ladies. Enjoy your stay in Washington." Then he and del Rio left through the side door.

Susan Caldwell sighed. "I'm sorry you had to hear that," she apologized. "Alejandro can be very rude."

"What exactly is he objecting to?" Nancy asked, puzzled. "Don't the museums in Mexico have any pre-Columbian art?"

"Of course they do," Susan Caldwell said. "The national museum in Mexico City has a splendid collection. But that's not what bothers him. I'm afraid I'd have to bore you with a lot of history to explain it properly."

"That's okay," Bess piped up. "We're used to being bored during history lessons."

George winced and then jabbed her cousin in the side.

Nancy chuckled. "Please tell us," she urged Susan.

"Well," the director began, "when the Spanish conquerors arrived in Mexico in the fifteenth century, they destroyed the culture of the Aztecs. Very little Aztec art remained once they were done. It's still a sore point for many Mexicans.

"In the late nineteenth century," she went on, "archaeologists discovered the ruins of the Maya and Olmec peoples—Indians who had lived in

Mexico before the Aztec empire. But as they dug up these artifacts, many of the sacred sites were robbed. This happened frequently during the time when the Cartwrights collected."

"So del Rio thinks some of the objects here were stolen from those sites?" Nancy asked.

Susan Caldwell shook her head. "No If they were, they would have been returned long ago," she said. "In the 1970s and 1980s, the United States and many Latin American countries agreed to stop the removal of pre-Columbian art from its native country. Experts also checked the origins of any pre-Columbian art that had already been removed. If something looked like a stolen piece, the art was sent back to its country of origin. The Cartwrights, though, had been very careful. Every piece they bought had a solid provenance."

"Provenance?" Bess echoed. "What do you mean?"

"It's like a pedigree. It tells where the art came from and who owned it," Susan Caldwell explained.

George still looked confused. "So what's del Rio's objection?" she asked.

"Alejandro is upset that the art was removed at all," Susan said. "Mexican nationalists—many of them of Indian descent, like Alejandro—bitterly resent the Spanish conquistadors who destroyed their art centuries ago. And they say that the American art collectors are like modern-day conquistadors, taking away the rest of Mexico's artistic heritage."

"What is this carving Beech Hill has just acquired?" Nancy asked.

"Oh, it's very special," Susan said enthusiastically. "It's a carving of the face of Lord Pacal, the ancient king of Palenque, one of the most prominent Mayan cities. The ancient Maya believed that it held the king's spirit. It was a sacred object."

"It must have been very expensive," Nancy commented.

Susan smiled. "Let's just say it was in the million-dollar range," she said. "It's rare and quite beautiful. And yes, its provenance checks out clean."

"Can we see it?" Nancy asked, intrigued.

The museum director thought for a moment. "I don't see why not," she finally said. "It's downstairs, locked in a storage case. Actually, I haven't seen it myself since we purchased it."

She led the girls to the door where Henrik van der Hune and Alejandro del Rio had exited. They all went down a set of narrow stairs and passed through a maze of gray-carpeted hallways.

Susan finally stopped at a plain black metal door. She pulled a set of keys from her skirt pocket, chose one, and fit it into the keyhole. The door swung open.

When Susan flipped on an overhead light, Nancy noticed they were in a square room. Two of the walls were fitted with floor-to-ceiling shelves for

9

holding pottery, sculpture, and other artifacts. There was also a massive storage case with lots of drawers and a long wooden table.

Susan crossed to the storage case. She scanned the labels on the drawers, then inserted another key into the tiny lock on one drawer. Pulling it out gently, she reached in and removed a well-worn cardboard gift box about the size of a deck of cards.

"Not the most attractive packaging in the world," Susan admitted with a smile, "but it serves the purpose. Isn't it hard to believe that something so valuable could be this small?"

With a flourish, she swept the lid off the box. "Here he is—Lord Pacal!"

The girls crowded around in anticipation, eager to see the priceless carving of the king. But as Susan Caldwell tilted the box for them to see inside, Nancy let out a loud gasp.

Aside from some lumpy cotton, the box was empty.

Lord Pacal was gone.

2

The Scarlet Handprint

"The carving is missing?" Susan Caldwell cried. "It can't be!" She flew back to the storage drawer and began to poke around inside.

"Maybe it fell out," she muttered. She reached her hand deeper into the drawer. When she pulled out her hand again, she was clutching something in her palm.

"What did you find?" Nancy asked.

"I don't know." Susan slowly opened her fingers. Lying in her palm was a small square of folded paper.

"It looks like a note," George said.

With trembling fingers, Susan opened the small square.

The paper was covered with black handwritten

characters unlike any Nancy had ever seen before. In the center of the unfolded sheet was an ominous-looking bloodred handprint.

Susan pointed to the black characters. "These are Mayan glyphs," she said in a dazed voice. "Each one stands for a word."

"Can you read what it says?" Nancy asked.

The director shook her head. "There are some scholars who are experts at reading Mayan glyphs. Unfortunately, I'm not one of them."

"What about the handprint?" Nancy asked. "Do you know what that means?"

Susan shuddered. "I'm not sure. It looks like blood, doesn't it?"

"That handprint sure is gruesome," Bess agreed, her eyes wide.

"Let's make sure none of us touches anything in here," Nancy warned. "The police will want this room just as it was when we entered."

Susan gave Nancy a curious look. "Do you know something about police investigations?"

"Nancy's got quite a reputation as a detective back in River Heights," Bess declared.

"You really solve mysteries?" the museum director exclaimed. "Well, I guess I shouldn't be surprised—you *are* Carson's daughter."

"I've solved a few cases," Nancy admitted modestly. "But an art theft like this should involve the police. We'd better call them."

Susan Caldwell nodded in agreement. But before

12

heading for the phone, she reached out and grabbed Nancy's hand. "Please tell me you'll help, too," she said urgently. "This statue was my responsibility—I have to see that it's returned to the museum."

"Sure," Nancy said, a little surprised at Susan's reaction. "As long as the police know I'm involved."

The director's face lit up. "Of course. I'll call the police now. Would you mind staying here until I return?"

The girls agreed, and Susan hurried back up the stairs.

"Well, so much for a nice relaxing vacation," Bess groaned. "I should have known: where Nancy Drew goes, mystery follows. We'll never get in any sightseeing now."

Nancy smiled at her friend's good-natured complaint. "We've got to help Susan, Bess. She's my dad's friend."

"I can't believe the statue was stolen," George remarked. "The security seems pretty tight around here."

Nancy nodded and began a quick check of the room. There were no signs of forced entry at the door or near the drawer where the carving was stored. A quick scan of the glossy linoleum floor didn't reveal any clues either.

"When the police come, they'll dust for fingerprints," Nancy remarked. "But I bet they won't find any. This theft seems well planned—the thief even left his calling card." She pointed to the mysterious note lying on the table.

"That thing gives me the creeps," Bess said. "I wonder what the handprint means." She hesitated. "Then again, maybe I don't want to know."

Susan returned a few minutes later and announced that the police were on their way.

"It doesn't look like anyone forced his way in," Nancy told her. "Who has keys to this room?"

"Just me," Susan replied, "and Henrik van der Hune, the curator you met earlier."

"No one else?" Nancy asked. Susan shook her head. "What about the cleaning people?"

"When they come, either Henrik or I stand outside," Susan explained. "It's awkward, but there's no way around it. The museum can't afford to lose something as valuable as the carving."

"Do you keep a set of spare keys anywhere?" Nancy asked.

Susan shook her head again. "Only Henrik and I have keys," she repeated.

Before Nancy could ask about who might have a motive to steal the carving, the door flew open.

"Susan! One of the guards just told me!" Henrik van der Hune stood in the doorway, looking distraught. "Is it true?"

"I'm afraid it is, Henrik," Susan admitted. "The carving is gone."

14

"But how?" He looked completely baffled.

"We don't know," she replied. "The police should be here any minute."

A deep voice came from behind van der Hune: "Excuse me." A tall, heavyset man in plain dark clothes pushed past the curator and entered the room. "Mrs. Caldwell?" he asked. "Detective Briscoe of the District Police. Your assistant sent me down here."

"Thanks for coming so quickly, Detective." The museum director shook his hand.

"You've got quite a crowd in here," Detective Briscoe commented. "Any way we can clear this room?"

"I'll wait in my office," van der Hune said.

Bess and George left the room after him.

"I'd like my friend Nancy Drew to stay," Susan Caldwell told Briscoe. "She's a detective."

Briscoe glanced at Nancy, a smirk creeping across his face. "A detective?" he asked. "Really?"

Nancy nodded and smiled politely, trying to hide her annoyance. She was used to police officers thinking that a teenager couldn't do much more than talk on the phone or shop at the mall. "I've solved quite a few mysteries back in River Heights, my hometown," she said.

Detective Briscoe shrugged. "I doubt you've ever been involved in something like this," he said.

Nancy simmered as he turned back to question

15

Susan Caldwell. Who did the detective think he was? She had been involved in many cases as serious as this one.

The detective suddenly noticed the piece of paper covered with the glyphs and the handprint. "Did you find this here?" he asked.

Susan nodded and told him how she had discovered that the carving was missing.

Briscoe reached into his jacket pocket, pulled out tweezers and a plastic evidence bag, and deftly slipped the note inside without touching it. Nancy knew he'd take it back to the lab for chemical analysis of the paper, ink, and the handprint. She then listened as Detective Briscoe asked Susan some of the same questions Nancy had already asked her.

Briscoe's final question was the one she'd wanted to ask Susan before they were interrupted.

"Do you know anyone who'd like to add the carving to their collection?"

The museum director shook her head. "It wasn't well known that we had it here," she said. "We'd only just bought it."

Briscoe nodded and snapped shut his notepad. "Do you have a photo of the carving?" he asked. "It helps to know what we're looking for."

"If you'll come up to my office, I'll be happy to give you one," Susan replied. "Nancy, come with us," she added.

As the three of them filed out of the room, Briscoe stopped to stick a length of yellow tape marked Crime Scene: No Trespassing across the doorframe.

"The forensics guy will be here in an hour to dust the room for fingerprints. He'll do a thorough inspection for any other evidence we might have missed," the detective explained. He grinned at Nancy. "Unless you have dusting equipment in your detective kit."

She forced herself to smile and didn't say anything. Obviously Detective Briscoe didn't take her at all seriously. Now she was more determined than ever to work on the case.

Nancy followed Susan Caldwell and the detective down the hallway and up a second set of stairs. The stairway led to a carpeted hallway lined with small offices. As they approached she noticed Henrik van der Hune stick his head out of a doorway. When he saw them, he popped back in as if he were avoiding them.

That's strange, Nancy thought. What does he have to hide?

The museum director's office had a big bay window overlooking Beech Hill's grand gardens. An elegant rosewood desk sat in front of the window.

Susan leaned over the desk and picked up her phone. "Sally, I need a picture from the photo archives." She paused. "Yes, Lord Pacal." She listened for a minute more and then hung up with a sigh.

"Word's out already," she groaned. "Detective, Sally says you told her to summon everyone on staff to the lunchroom."

He nodded. "I'm going to need to talk to them one by one," he explained. "Standard procedure. And I'll get samples of their handwriting to compare to this note." He patted his pocket where he had put the evidence bag with the note in it.

"Detective Briscoe, may I make a copy of that note?" Susan asked. "I'd like to take it to someone who reads glyphs."

Briscoe hesitated. "This note hasn't been dusted for fingerprints," he said. "Let me get it to the lab first, then I'll get a photocopy over to you."

"Fair enough," Susan replied.

A moment later a young woman entered and handed Susan a manila folder.

"Thanks, Sally." The museum director opened the folder and handed Briscoe a photograph. "Here he is—Lord Pacal."

Nancy looked over Briscoe's shoulder. The color photograph showed an intricate small carving cut out of greenish stone. A ruler laid next to it in the photo indicated that the piece was not quite three inches tall. Without the ruler, Nancy would have thought the carving was much larger.

She carefully studied the image of the king. Lord Pacal had been depicted with a sloping forehead, a strong, straight nose, and full lips. He looks haughty and powerful, Nancy thought, and also vaguely familiar. Where had she seen that face before?

Briscoe shoved the photo into his pocket, then asked Susan to come to the lunchroom for the questioning.

"Of course," she answered. She turned to Nancy, asking, "Can you come back tomorrow morning?" Behind Briscoe's back, she shot Nancy a pleading glance.

"Sure," Nancy agreed.

Back at the hotel that night, Nancy and her friends ate dinner in the restaurant with Carson Drew. Over crab cakes and tossed green salad they filled him in on Nancy's newest case.

"It seems to me there are two suspects," Nancy speculated out loud.

"One is the Mexican diplomat, Alejandro del Rio," George piped up. "He certainly has a motive."

Bess sighed. "He sure is handsome, too."

George rolled her eyes. "He's only about ten years too old for you, Bess," she pointed out. "Are you into art thieves now?"

"No," Bess retorted. "I'm just making an observation about a prime suspect."

19

Nancy grinned at the cousins' exchange. "That's enough, you two."

"What about the curator, Henrik van der Hune?" George asked, turning back to Nancy. "He's the only other person with a key to the storage room."

"That nice man with the accent?" Bess chimed in. "He seemed so charming."

"He's also sympathetic to del Rio's cause," Nancy reminded Bess. "And he avoided Susan and me in the hallway after the theft. That sure looked suspicious."

Carson Drew smiled at his daughter. "I'm glad Susan asked you to help. Losing a valuable piece of art like that is a disaster for any museum director— she could even lose her job."

Nancy nodded. "She seemed very upset."

"I'm sure you can get to the bottom of things," her father went on.

Nancy certainly hoped so, even if Detective Briscoe didn't agree with her father's high opinion of her.

The next morning Nancy, Bess, and George walked down the hallway to Susan Caldwell's office. Ahead, Nancy saw Henrik van der Hune step out of a doorway again—and just as quickly jump back in.

She told her friends to wait for her in the director's office. "I'll be right there," she promised.

She entered the doorway where she'd seen van

der Hune. Inside the office he was sitting behind his desk, looking at some papers.

"Hi, Mr. van der Hune," Nancy said brightly. "It's awful about the carving being stolen, isn't it?"

The curator nodded, barely looking up. "Yes."

"Susan Caldwell has asked me to help investigate," Nancy commented matter-of-factly.

"Good luck to you," van der Hune mumbled. "I've heard you're quite a detective."

She lingered in his doorway. The curator clearly wasn't interested in talking with her, but Nancy was determined to get some information out of him.

"Does Alejandro del Rio have any personal reason for being so attached to pre-Columbian art?" she asked.

At that van der Hune finally looked up. "He loves his country. And he feels very strongly about the repatriation of pre-Columbian art objects."

"Repatriation?" Nancy repeated. "What's that?"

"Returning art to its native land," the curator explained. "As we were discussing yesterday, it has become quite an issue in the art world."

"Is it an issue with you?" Nancy asked.

Van der Hune gave her a sharp look. "I understand both points of view," he answered, sounding annoyed. "Now, if you don't mind, I'd like to return to my work."

Nancy knew she had gotten all the information she could from him now. "I do have some more questions," she said. "Can I come back later?"

"Of course, anytime," he replied with a wave of his hand. "I'll be here all day."

"Thank you," Nancy replied.

When she entered Susan Caldwell's office, the director stood up and reached for her coat. "Oh, hi, Nancy," she said. "I was just telling George and Bess that I'm taking you all to the Mexican consulate. They have a wonderful display of carvings that are similar to the one that was stolen. I thought you might like to see them."

"You bet," Nancy said. "I'd like to learn all I can about pre-Columbian art."

Susan led them out of Beech Hill and to her car. They drove to the Mexican consulate, a yellow stone building on 16th Street. Immediately beyond the entrance was a large room with several artifacts displayed in glass cases.

The girls walked from carving to carving as Susan pointed out the different kinds of greenstone from which the objects were carved. She also explained some of the symbols the Maya used to represent their gods: the jaguar, the serpent, and a number of birds.

Later, as they were leaving the consulate, Nancy glanced back at the building, wondering where Alejandro del Rio's office might be. Then something she spotted out of the corner of her eye made her stop in her tracks.

Henrik van der Hune was turning onto a pathway that ran up the side of the consulate. He moved

22

quickly, his head down. Tucked under his arm was a small package.

What's he doing here? Nancy wondered. And what was in the package under his arm? But then, before Nancy could say anything or try to stop him, van der Hune ducked into a side entrance and disappeared from view.

3

Danger in the Garden

"I just saw Henrik van der Hune!" Nancy grabbed Susan Caldwell's arm and pointed to the side door.

Susan squinted in the bright sun. "Where?" she asked.

"He went in through that entrance," Nancy explained. "The odd thing is, he told me earlier that he was going to be at Beech Hill all day. He had a package with him, too."

Susan looked surprised. "I've known Henrik a long time. Surely you don't suspect *him?*"

"I'm just curious about him," Nancy told the director cautiously. She knew it was natural for Susan to trust someone she had known for so long. But she might be trusting the wrong person.

"I'm sure Henrik is here to see someone about

the upcoming exhibition," Susan assured Nancy. "Maybe some question arose after he spoke to you. There are so many details involved in mounting an exhibition."

Nancy nodded, staying silent. Until she had further evidence, she wouldn't say anything more about van der Hune to Susan.

On the way back to Beech Hill, the four of them discussed the stolen carving. "Susan, I meant to ask you," George piped up from the backseat, "who was this Lord Pacal anyway? Was he a real guy?"

"Oh, yes," Susan replied. "Inscriptions found on other objects at Palenque revealed that he was born in 603 and came to the throne when he was twelve."

Bess gasped. "Isn't that a little young?"

The museum director laughed. "Not in Mayan culture," she said. "He ruled for sixty-eight years, turning Palenque into one of the leading cities of its time. But after his death, Mayan civilization began to fade."

"Why?" George asked.

"No one really knows," Susan answered. "We suspect its population increased too rapidly and outgrew its food supply. Or maybe battles between rival cities killed off many people. Neither explanation has been proven yet."

"When was this image of Lord Pacal carved?" Nancy asked.

"We're not sure of that either," Susan admitted.

"He looks pretty young in the carving, so we think it might have been made to commemorate his marriage to the Lady Ahpo-Hel."

"What's the carving made of?" Bess asked. "You keep calling it greenstone, but it sure looks like jade to me."

"The Maya carved a number of different kinds of stone—jade, jadeite, serpentine," Susan answered. "But all were some shade of green. The Maya themselves called them all greenstone, so that's the term we art historians use."

"Are the jades we saw at the consulate as valuable as the one of Lord Pacal?" Nancy asked.

The museum director shook her head. "Lord Pacal is unique," she said. "The carving has enormous historical value because Lord Pacal was king of a great Mayan city, and of course, the carving itself is beautifully done. That's why it had such a high price tag."

Susan steered the car into Beech Hill's parking lot. As they climbed out of the car, she glanced at her watch. "We're just in time for my meeting with Taylor Sinclair. He's the art dealer who sold Lord Pacal to us," she told the girls. "Detective Briscoe wanted to speak with him, and I've arranged to see Taylor afterward."

She glanced at Nancy. "I'd like you to meet him, too. He knows everyone in the world of pre-Columbian art. He may have some ideas about who's behind the theft."

26

In the lobby of Beech Hill, Nancy spotted a silver-haired man in gray slacks and a navy blue blazer. He was leaning against the oak desk, chatting with several guards. Since the theft at Beech Hill, security had been tightened, Nancy noticed. Uniformed guards were everywhere.

"Taylor!" Susan exclaimed.

"My dear." Taylor Sinclair straightened up and clasped Susan's hand. "I am so sorry for your loss."

They hugged briefly.

"I hope Detective Briscoe didn't give you the third degree," Susan said to him.

Sinclair shrugged. "I emerged unscathed," he joked. He pretended to dust off his jacket.

"Don't make fun, Taylor," Susan chided him. "This is serious."

"Yes, I know," he replied. "And it happens more than we'd like to admit, doesn't it?"

"What happens?" Nancy put in.

Taylor Sinclair turned in her direction. "Art theft," he said, as if it should be obvious to everyone. "It happens all the time."

"This is Nancy Drew," Susan said, introducing her. "Nancy is a detective, Taylor. She's helping us investigate the theft."

Nancy winced as Susan finished making introductions all around. The fewer people who know what I'm doing, the better, she thought.

"So, you're a detective," Taylor Sinclair said,

27

fixing his blue eyes on her. "Do you have any suspects in the case?"

"Well, there are several people who don't think Beech Hill had a right to the carving," she said vaguely.

"Ah, the repatriation bunch." Sinclair rolled his eyes.

"You don't think they have a valid point?" Nancy asked him.

"Some of the pieces they're objecting to have been in this country for years," Sinclair said. "Whenever a major piece of pre-Columbian art comes on the market, they always sing the same song of woe. I've learned to ignore it."

He's not very sympathetic to Alejandro del Rio's cause, Nancy thought. She noticed that Susan looked surprised at Sinclair's attitude as well.

"Anyway, the provenance of the Lord Pacal carving is very secure," Sinclair said breezily. "The documents prove that."

"Would it be possible for me to see those documents?" Nancy asked.

"I don't see why not," Susan said. "I'll get them from Henrik's files."

"Henrik doesn't seem to be here," Sinclair informed Susan. "And Briscoe told me he'd searched high and low for those papers with no success. Luckily, I brought my own copies." Sinclair lifted his sleek leather attaché case. "But let's look at them in your office, Susan. It's getting a little noisy in here." He glanced scornfully over his shoulder at the chattering tour group that was beginning to fill the lobby.

As Susan and Sinclair started toward Susan's office, Nancy turned to Bess and George. "Why don't you guys take a walk through the galleries and gardens?" she suggested quietly. "See if you notice anything unusual."

The two girls nodded, then headed for the nearest gallery.

Nancy trotted after Susan and Taylor. In Susan's office, Taylor was placing a manila folder on her rosewood desk. He opened it and removed a piece of paper.

"This is the original bill of sale," he said, handing it to Nancy.

Nancy scanned it quickly. The letterhead was from a gallery in Los Angeles. The bill of sale was made out to a Mr. and Mrs. Petersen in Connecticut and dated 1955.

"Is the Los Angeles gallery still there?" Nancy asked.

"Unfortunately, no," Sinclair said.

That's a shame, Nancy thought. That probably meant she wouldn't be able to trace the history of the carving beyond the Petersens' ownership.

"What was the provenance of the piece before it reached the gallery?" she asked Sinclair.

Taylor Sinclair raised his eyebrows. "Smart question," he said. "It came into the country legally in the 1940s and was in private hands at first. Then the market for pre-Columbian art got hot, and the Los Angeles gallery acquired it."

"Who were the Petersens?" Nancy asked.

"They were well-known pre-Columbian art collectors," Sinclair explained. "They both died last year, and their estate quietly began to sell pieces from the collection."

He pulled out another piece of paper. It was a letter to Sinclair from a Connecticut lawyer's office, dated earlier in the year. It informed him that the Petersens' collection was up for sale.

"I worked with the estate on a number of sales to different parties," Sinclair said. "The collection was too big and too expensive to interest a single buyer."

Next he showed her a letter from the lawyers about a small carving in the collection. Stapled to it was a copy of the photograph of Lord Pacal she'd seen. "One of the best pieces was the Lord Pacal carving," Sinclair continued. "I knew Beech Hill was right for it. Fortunately, they were the highest bidder."

He showed her the record of the sale to Beech Hill. As Susan Caldwell had indicated, the price for the carving was well over a million dollars.

"Do you get paid for handling the sale?" Nancy asked him.

"A ten percent commission—that's standard in the art world," said Sinclair. He closed the folder and placed it in his briefcase. "There are some unscrupulous dealers out there, but I think Susan will tell you I'm not one of them."

Susan nodded. "We've worked with Taylor for years."

"Well, I've got to be on my way," Sinclair said, picking up his briefcase. He turned to Susan. "Let me know if you need me for anything," he added.

"I will," she promised as she showed him out of her office.

Taylor Sinclair's presentation of the documents had been very professional, Nancy thought. Still, there was something about him she didn't like.

"You mentioned that you knew someone who could decipher the writing on that piece of paper we found in the drawer," she reminded Susan.

"Oh, yes—John Riggs," Susan said. "He's an archaeologist at the Museum of Natural History. I've made an appointment with him for you this afternoon at two." She handed Nancy a photocopy of the thief's threatening note. "Detective Briscoe sent this over this morning. He'll have the report on it this afternoon. I'd go to see Riggs with you, but the insurance adjusters want to talk to me this afternoon. Lord Pacal was insured, thank goodness. If he isn't found soon, we'll have to file a claim."

She briefly told Nancy how to find Rigg's office in the museum. Nancy promised to call her afterward and then left.

As she passed through the hallway to the lobby,

31

Nancy gazed out at Beech Hill's front lawn through a set of French doors. Henrik van der Hune was walking toward the entrance, still carrying the package he'd had at the consulate.

Then she saw him stop in his tracks. Taylor Sinclair strolled into view.

As the two men started talking, Nancy stood still, watching alertly. Judging from the expressions on their faces, especially Henrik van der Hune's, this was not a friendly discussion.

Van der Hune and Sinclair exchanged more words, then Sinclair walked away briskly, heading for his car. Van der Hune watched Sinclair's departure, an angry expression on his face. Then he stalked off into the gardens of Beech Hill.

Nancy dashed out of the mansion and toward the gardens. She had a lot of questions for van der Hune—she couldn't let the curator get away.

She pushed through the wooden gate and found herself in a formal flower garden enclosed by tall stone walls. Van der Hune sat on a low wooden bench across the garden. His head hung down, and he seemed deep in thought.

Nancy called out to him from across the garden. "Mr. van der Hune?"

He flashed her an irritated look.

"There's something I'd like to ask you." Nancy started toward him. But before she could reach him, a movement above his head caught her eye. A stone statue of an armless woman teetered on the wall above van der Hune.

"Watch out!" Nancy shouted.

She raced over to him, but before she could reach him, the statue toppled off the wall and struck the back of van der Hune's neck.

With a horrible moan, Henrik van der Hune pitched forward. He fell down face first, the statue's shattered pieces scattered around him.

4

The Code Is Cracked

Nancy knelt at Henrik van der Hune's side. She was relieved to see that he was still breathing. She put her fingers on his wrist and felt a faint pulse.

She stood up and shouted for help. A few minutes later, Bess and George burst through an ivy-covered arch on the other side of the enclosed garden.

"We were in the rose garden when we heard you shout," George said. Then she looked down at van der Hune and gasped.

"A statue struck him, and he's unconscious," Nancy said grimly. "Bess, can you run back to Susan's office and have her call an ambulance."

Without a word, Bess turned and ran out of the garden.

Nancy and George bent over the unconscious man. "What were you doing here?" George asked.

"I followed van der Hune," Nancy told her. "I saw him through a window, having an argument with Taylor Sinclair. Then van der Hune came in here."

"What were they fighting about?" George asked.

"That's what I wanted to find out," Nancy replied. "I was also about to ask him why he was at the consulate this morning."

"Is that the package he was carrying this morning?" George pointed to a pale gray envelope lying on the ground under van der Hune.

"Good eyes, George!" Nancy said. She stooped to ease out the envelope without moving the unconscious man. A quick glance inside told Nancy exactly what she had.

"The provenance documents for Lord Pacal," she announced. "Taylor Sinclair said they were missing when Detective Briscoe wanted to see them. I wonder why van der Hune took them to the Mexican consulate."

Before George could reply, Susan and Bess rushed toward them.

"Oh no!" Susan cried, falling to her knees at Henrik's side.

Nancy quickly described what had happened.

"This statue fell?" Susan asked, shocked. She glanced over at the broken chunks on the grass. "I can't imagine how! It's bolted to the wall."

Just then the wail of a siren pierced the air, and Susan jumped up and ran back toward the mansion to direct the paramedics.

A few minutes later, the ambulance attendants laid van der Hune on a stretcher and took him to the waiting ambulance.

Susan hopped in the back. "I'm going to the hospital with him," she told Nancy. "Don't forget your appointment with John Riggs. And call Detective Briscoe to get the results of those lab reports on the note. We've got to get to the bottom of this before anyone else gets hurt."

So I'm not the only one who thinks that this wasn't an accident, Nancy thought as the ambulance drove away. She turned to Bess and George. "Let's take a look at that wall."

Inside the garden she handed the provenance documents to George. Then she jumped up onto the bench where van der Hune had been sitting and examined the top of the wall.

"Just as I thought!" she exclaimed a minute later.

"What is it?" asked Bess.

"The statue was held to the wall with iron brackets," Nancy said, "and they've both been unscrewed." She pulled the brackets off the wall and showed them to Bess and George. "Someone deliberately pushed that statue off the wall."

"But who?" George asked.

"That's what we're going to have to find out,"

Nancy said. "You two didn't see anyone suspicious hanging around the garden, did you?"

"No," Bess answered. "Lots of tourists are walking around the grounds, but no one seemed unusual."

Nancy glanced at her watch. She had an hour or so before her appointment with John Riggs. "Let's go back to Susan's office and call Detective Briscoe," she suggested. "If the lab reports are in, they might tell us something. Then we'll get some lunch before we see Riggs."

Back in Susan's office, Nancy phoned the police station.

"I can't share the results of the lab report with you," Briscoe stated gruffly when he heard why she was calling.

"But Susan *asked* me to call," Nancy persisted. "She had to go to the hospital with her curator." Briefly, she described what had happened to Henrik van der Hune. "I think the statue was deliberately pushed off that wall," she finished.

Briscoe snorted. "Don't let your imagination run away with you. This is an art theft, plain and simple."

"Fine," she shot back, annoyed that Briscoe wouldn't even consider her theory. "Can you at least give me the lab results so they're waiting for Susan when she returns?"

Briscoe clucked his tongue in exasperation.

"Okay, okay. Here it is. The ink is your standard bottled fountain pen ink, and the paper is good-quality drawing paper. Either one of those would be available at any art store. It's the red handprint that's oddball," he added.

"Why?" Nancy asked.

"The lab's chemical analysis says it's made of mercuric sulfide," he responded.

"Which is . . .?" Nancy prodded.

"A powdered mineral," Briscoe said. "The lab report suggests it was mixed with water to make a paste. Then someone dipped his hand in it and left his handprint on the paper."

"His?" Nancy echoed. "How do you know it wasn't a woman?"

"The print is large enough so that it's almost certainly a man's," Briscoe informed her. "But he was clever enough to smudge the fingerprints so we can't read them. And there aren't any prints on the note itself either."

Briscoe went on to tell Nancy that the storage room was completely clean as well. There wasn't a shred of evidence. "Smart thief," he added.

For the first time since she'd met him, Nancy found herself agreeing with Briscoe.

"Tell Mrs. Caldwell I've notified the international art authorities," Briscoe went on. "About all they'll do at this point is put art dealers on notice that the carving is missing in case it shows up anywhere. But the authorities figure it's probably already in the hands of some private collector by now."

"I'm going to see John Riggs, an archaeologist at the Museum of Natural History," she told him. "Mrs. Caldwell says he'll be able to decode those Maya glyphs. Maybe that will tell us something."

"If it leads you anywhere, let me know," Briscoe remarked. "I'll follow up on my interviews with the staff yesterday. But if you want to know what I think, that carving's gone for good. And we can't spend a lot of time and money looking for something that no one will ever find."

Nancy said goodbye and hung up the phone with a sigh. "Briscoe doesn't sound very hopeful about finding the carving," she told Bess and George.

"Then Briscoe doesn't know you," Bess said loyally. "Is there a mystery you haven't solved yet?"

This brought a small smile to Nancy's face. "Not that I know of," she admitted. "Okay, let's go."

George held up the gray envelope that contained the provenance documents. "Should we leave these on Susan's desk?"

Nancy thought for a moment. "No, I don't think she'd want them left lying around. Let's take them. They'll be safer with us."

After a quick lunch at an outdoor café in George-town, Nancy and her friends drove downtown to the Museum of Natural History. On the way, Nancy tried to fit together the few available pieces of the puzzle.

"Really, all I have are questions!" she burst out in frustration to Bess and George. "Why was Henrik van der Hune at the consulate this morning? What was he arguing about with Taylor Sinclair? And who tried to harm him?"

"Now that van der Hune's in the hospital, he's not exactly available for questioning," George pointed out. "Maybe he knew something and the thief wanted to quiet him."

Nancy nodded as she pulled the car into a parking lot next to the museum. The three friends climbed out of the car and headed for the museum.

The Museum of Natural History filled an entire block, its solid granite facade punctuated with heavy columns and wide, tall windows. In front of the museum, a life-size sculpture of a dinosaur was swarming with climbing, giggling children.

The girls hurried up the steps of the building, weaving in and out of the crowd. Inside the main rotunda, they stood in a sea of people, mostly parents and their children. Nancy quickly spotted an information desk off to one side and went over to get a floor plan. They quickly located Riggs's office on the map and headed toward it, through a maze of galleries filled with Native American relics. Finally they turned down a narrow hallway off the far end of a gallery.

"Riggs's office should be right here," Nancy announced.

She stepped up to a doorway, peered in, and saw a slightly built, sandy-haired man sitting behind a plain black metal desk. "John Riggs?" Nancy asked.

The man stood and offered her a freckled hand. "Ms. Drew," he welcomed her. "Come in."

Nancy introduced Bess and George, then they all sat on folding chairs he set up in front of his desk.

"I guess Mrs. Caldwell told you about the theft of Lord Pacal?" Nancy began.

John Riggs leaned back in his chair and put his feet up on his desk. "It's a shame, isn't it?" he said in a cheerful voice. "They spent so much money for it. If *this* museum had bought it, it would be here now. Safe."

Nancy couldn't hide her surprise. "Your museum bid on the carving, too?"

"Oh, yes, Taylor Sinclair had quite a little bidding war going," he said, sounding bitter. "But Beech Hill won. That's how it goes, I suppose— they've got all the money."

"Is there a pre-Columbian collection in this museum?" Nancy asked.

Riggs nodded. "Yes, and the carving would have filled a major gap in it," he said. "It also would have been seen by many more people if it were here."

Ignoring his dig at Beech Hill, Nancy pulled the copy of the thief's note out of her file. "Susan

41

Caldwell says you can decipher this." Nancy handed it to him. "Can you?"

John Riggs swung down his feet, took the photocopy from Nancy, and placed it on his desk. "I may be one of the few people who can," he said.

He pulled out a lined pad and began to follow the glyphs, writing down words as he went.

A few moments later Riggs raised his head. His eyes met Nancy's. "The message is not pleasant," he stated grimly. "It threatens anyone who tries to find the carving with death—by dismemberment."

"Dismemberment?" Bess cried. "Doesn't that mean chopping off legs and arms?"

Nancy nodded. "I'm afraid so."

"Whoever wrote this knows their glyphs," John Riggs went on. "And the message was taken from an old Mayan inscription. The handprint is an interesting touch," he added.

"The police lab says the handprint was made out of a substance called mercuric sulfide," Nancy said. "Does that mean anything to you?"

Riggs nodded. "Mercuric sulfide is the scientific name for a red powder commonly called cinnabar," he explained. "The Maya thought it was precious, and they often rubbed it into their carvings. The red powder made the lines of the carving stand out. I don't have any, otherwise I'd show you what I mean."

Nancy pulled the photo of Lord Pacal from her file folder. "Is this what you mean?" she asked. She pointed to a red crust inside some of the curves that outlined Lord Pacal's face.

"Yes," Riggs said. "Only the most important objects were rubbed with cinnabar, of course. Lord Pacal's image was sacred to the Maya."

"So sacred that someone might want to steal it back for their country?" Nancy asked.

Riggs gave her a questioning look. "Perhaps," he murmured.

Nancy looked intently at Lord Pacal's face again. Suddenly it came to her—the person whom he reminded her of.

At that moment, Nancy heard the shuffle of someone's feet in the doorway behind her. She turned and saw the man whose face she'd just been thinking about—

Alejandro del Rio!

5

Splashdown

Alejandro del Rio stood in the doorway, staring at Nancy. On his face was a startled expression. Abruptly he wheeled around and ran back down the narrow hallway.

Nancy turned back to John Riggs. "Do you know that man?"

"He's an attaché with the Mexican consulate," Riggs replied. "I see him at cultural events around town. But I wasn't expecting him here."

"It looked like he wasn't expecting us, either," Nancy said. "Anyway, thanks for your help with the glyphs." Rising to leave, she scooped up the papers and photo and stuffed them back in the gray envelope. "We'll be in touch."

Out in the hallway, Nancy turned to her friends. "Have either of you noticed how much he looks like Lord Pacal?"

"That's true," George said thoughtfully. Then her face wrinkled up into a puzzled frown. "So what does that mean?"

Nancy shrugged. "I don't know," she said truthfully. "Maybe it's just a coincidence. On the other hand, we know how much he resents the fact that Beech Hill owns the carving. The two things could be connected."

"He took off when he realized it was you, Nancy," Bess remarked. "He sure looked like he has something to hide."

Nancy pulled out the floor plan of the museum and studied it carefully. Del Rio had probably left the museum if he wanted to avoid her, she reasoned, and there were only two possible exits. Nancy suspected he would take the quickest way out—the main entrance.

Weaving through the crowded galleries, Nancy and her friends soon reached the crowded main rotunda. The girls burst outside in time to see del Rio at the bottom of the steps, hailing a cab. As Nancy sprinted down the stairs, a cab pulled up and he hopped in. "The Jefferson Memorial," she heard him say to the driver, and the cab sped away.

Another cab pulled up to the curb right behind it. There was no time to collect their rental car.

45

Nancy and her friends jumped in the cab. "The Jefferson Memorial," Nancy told the driver. "And hurry, please."

"Why would del Rio be going there?" George asked as the cab hurtled along Madison Drive.

"I doubt it's to sightsee," Nancy remarked. Outside the sidewalks were packed with people.

"Is Washington always this crowded?" Nancy asked the cabbie.

"Today's the Cherry Blossom Parade down Constitution Avenue," he replied. "It happens every year when the cherry trees are in bloom, and every year it gets crazier." The light turned green, but not a car moved.

"A traffic jam!" Bess wailed. "We'll never catch up to Alejandro now!"

"Don't worry," George said evenly. "He's in the same traffic jam we are."

Finally, the cab inched forward and turned onto the 12th Street Expressway. A tall, white granite obelisk came into view on their right.

"I can never get all these monuments straight," George confessed. "Is that the Jefferson Memorial?"

"That's the Washington Monument," Nancy said. "The Jefferson Memorial has a dome on top."

"It's the one you see on the back of a nickel," Bess added. "And the Lincoln Memorial's the rectangular building with columns all along the side—it's the one shown on the penny."

46

"Bravo, Bess," Nancy said. "You've been doing your research, all right."

"Well, the way this case is going, the only time I *will* get to see the sights is on the back of money," Bess teased.

Soon they were within sight of the Tidal Basin, a large man-made pool that drained off the Potomac. Blossoming cherry trees lined its perimeter.

When the cab pulled into the parking lot behind the Jefferson Memorial, Nancy paid the fare and the girls hopped out quickly.

Crowds swarmed the path that led to the front of the monument.

"How are we ever going to find del Rio?" Nancy moaned.

"Why don't we break up and look," George suggested. "We can meet back here in half an hour."

"Good idea," Nancy agreed.

Bess and George went to either side of the monument to explore the crowded sidewalks around the Tidal Basin, and Nancy headed up the wide marble stairs.

Once she'd reached the rotunda, Nancy gazed around in wonder at the perfect classical proportions of the building. It reminded her of Monticello, the home in Virginia that Jefferson had designed for himself.

A tall statue of Jefferson himself sat at the center of the rotunda. A large crowd milled in front of the statue of one of the greatest men of American history.

Nancy scanned the mass of tourists. Behind a set of twins, she saw a tall dark man staring intently at the statue of Jefferson. It was Alejandro del Rio!

Quickly she slipped through the crowd toward him. Before she could reach him, he turned around and jogged down the stairs to the edge of the Tidal Basin. Nancy threaded her way through the crowd to follow him, hoping he hadn't seen her.

At the water's edge, del Rio turned to his right and walked along the path. Pink cherry blossoms arched over his head.

Nancy followed him at a discreet distance.

Suddenly he stopped at a bench. A thin, dark-clothed man sat there, his face mostly hidden by the pulled-up hood of his sweatshirt. Del Rio spoke to him for a few minutes. Then the man on the bench rose and left. Del Rio continued along the path.

Quickening her pace, Nancy caught up with del Rio.

"Hi!" she said brightly.

At the sound of her voice he turned. "Oh," he said. "Miss Drew."

"Nancy," she said, smiling. "So what were you doing at John Riggs's office?"

Del Rio picked up his pace. "He's someone I know," he replied.

"Then why did you leave without talking to him?" Nancy persisted.

"I suddenly realized I had somewhere else to be," he snapped.

"Like here?" Nancy said. "To talk to that man on the bench?"

He stopped midstep. "What man?" Then he threw his head back and laughed. "Oh, that man! All he wanted to know was whether I had any spare change."

"It took you quite a while to tell him no," Nancy pointed out.

Del Rio shrugged. "Some people won't take no for an answer," he replied.

He began to walk again. Nancy kept pace.

"I know that you don't approve of Beech Hill's having the carving of Lord Pacal," she began.

Del Rio turned to her with a furious look. "Look, is there a point to this questioning?"

Nancy softened her voice. "I wanted to hear more about why you feel so strongly about the stolen carving belonging in Mexico."

"Why should I explain my thoughts to you?" He narrowed his eyes.

"Because I'm investigating the theft of the carving of Lord Pacal," Nancy told him. "Any information I gather helps."

Del Rio paused for a moment. "It should never have been at Beech Hill in the first place," he stated angrily. "It belongs in its homeland. Frankly, I wish I *had* stolen the carving myself. At least I would make sure it ended up in the right hands."

49

What did that mean? Nancy wondered. Did del Rio know something about the theft? Or was he trying to throw her off the track?

She drew a deep breath. "*Did* you steal the carving?" she asked boldly.

He halted in his tracks. "How dare you ask me that!" His face was twisted with rage.

"I won't know unless I ask," Nancy responded calmly. "You certainly have a motive for stealing it."

Del Rio waited a moment before he replied. "I may have a motive, but I am not a thief." With that, he strode off.

Nancy let him go. She knew there was no point in continuing the conversation. She had no evidence linking him to the theft—all she had was the unsettling feeling that he was keeping something from her.

She turned and walked slowly back to the memorial, still holding the gray envelope with the provenance documents under her arm. She could see Bess and George in the distance, sitting on the steps and looking around for her.

She started to wave to them when someone in the crowd behind her yelled, "Look out!"

She turned and saw a speeding bicycle bearing down on her. Pedaling furiously was a thin, dark-clothed man with a hooded sweatshirt—the same man del Rio had been talking to a few minutes earlier!

50

"Hey!" she yelled. She leapt onto the grass alongside the Tidal Basin.

The cyclist steared his bike onto the grass behind her. Swerving to the side, he reached with one hand for the gray envelope tucked under her arm. As Nancy yanked it out of his grasp, she lost her balance and toppled into the shallow water of the Tidal Basin. Frantically, she held the gray envelope above her head, out of the water.

Several tourists rushed over to help Nancy as the cyclist sped away. When she pulled herself up out of the pool, she was drenched from head to foot.

"Are you all right?" a kind-looking older man asked as she sat trying to catch her breath.

"I'm fine." She nodded.

"What nerve!" The older man harrumphed. "They ought to have licenses for bikes. That man practically ran you over!"

Nancy stood and felt water ooze out of her sneakers.

Bess and George rushed over. "Nancy!" Bess cried. "Are you okay?"

"I'm fine," Nancy told her friends. "Just drenched." She handed the gray envelope to Bess. "Here, keep this dry. And hold it close," she ordered. Nancy reached down to wring out the tail of her wet shirt.

George handed Nancy some tissues from a pocket pack. "These won't exactly dry you off," she said, "but they're better than nothing."

Nancy smiled her thanks and wiped her face dry.

"I saw the guy who did it," George went on. "He flew past us on his bike."

"Did you get a good look at him?" Nancy asked.

"He was thin and dark haired," George replied.

"How could you tell?" Nancy asked. "Didn't he have the hood of his sweatshirt pulled up?"

George nodded. "Yes, but his hair was sticking out." She smiled wryly. "I guess he didn't have time to comb it after knocking you into the basin."

Nancy quickly told her friends about what happened with Alejandro del Rio. "I'm sure the man who chased me was the man I saw del Rio talking to earlier."

Bess and George gasped.

"Why would he want to hurt you?" George asked.

"I don't think he wanted to hurt me," Nancy said. She pointed to the gray envelope Bess was holding. "That's what the guy on the bike was after. The provenance documents."

6

A Call in the Night

"Why would that man on the bicycle want the provenance documents?" George looked perplexed.

"I'm not sure," Nancy admitted. "But he was definitely trying to grab them. Obviously there's something in here that he wants badly."

As the girls reached the rear of the memorial, Nancy looked around for a cab.

"But what is his connection to Alejandro del Rio?" Bess asked.

Nancy shrugged. "Who knows? One thing's for sure—he wasn't just panhandling, as Alejandro said." A cab pulled up to the curb, and the girls climbed in.

"Where to, ladies?" the driver asked.

"Beech Hill," Nancy started to say, but George interrupted her.

"No way, Nancy. You need to change out of those wet clothes. We'll drop you off at the hotel first, and then Bess and I will go pick up the car at the museum parking lot."

Nancy suddenly realized how damp and chilled she felt. She readily agreed to George's plan.

The cab dropped off Nancy at the hotel. She hurried up to their room to shed her wet clothes, shower, and get dressed. Then, picking up the provenance documents, she went back to the lobby, where she'd agreed to meet George and Bess for afternoon tea.

Downstairs, in one of the lounge areas, waiters were rolling out large silver tea urns and trays heaped with small sandwiches, cookies, pastries, and cakes. Hotel guests and people dressed in business suits sat on the plump chairs and couches, sipping tea and eating the desserts. Nancy quickly found George and Bess sitting on a small sofa beside a low table. Bess bit into a chocolate eclair. "This is delicious," she pronounced. "From now on we're coming to tea every day—no matter how close we are to finding the thief!"

Nancy smiled at her friend. "No promises, Bess."

A waitress poured out a cup of hot tea as Nancy began pulling papers out of the gray envelope. "I'd better return these to Beech Hill as soon as we're finished with our tea," she said. "But first I want to figure out why that guy on the bike was so interested in them."

Bess and George looked on as Nancy scrutinized the papers.

"These seem to be the original papers that Taylor Sinclair photocopied," she remarked. "I don't see anything here I didn't see in his copies."

She studied the final sheet of paper—the bill of sale, which documented the museum's purchase of the carving.

"Hmm. The Petersens had the same zip code as my aunt who lives in Guilford, Connecticut," George noted. "They must have lived near her."

Carson Drew leaned over the back of their sofa. "Have a good day, girls?"

Nancy hopped up to give her father a hug. "How's your seminar going?" she asked.

"Fine," he replied. "I just came back to make some phone calls. How are you girls?"

Briefly, Nancy described the events of the day. Carson Drew listened closely as she went over everything that had happened. He agreed that Alejandro del Rio's behavior was suspicious, then sat thinking for a moment.

"It sounds as though the note left by the thief is the only real piece of evidence you have," he commented finally. "All these other things—van der Hune's argument with Sinclair, the falling statue, the man on the bike—might not be related to the theft at all."

Reluctantly Nancy agreed. Each of those things could be important, but the note was the only solid clue in the case.

Carson Drew's expression turned grave as he stood up to leave. "Please be careful, Nancy. People who leave notes like the one you found may not be playing games."

Nancy nodded. "Don't worry, Dad. I know what I'm doing."

He squeezed her hand. "Have fun, girls. I'll see you later."

George turned to Nancy and Bess. "Ready to go?"

Nancy nodded and stood. But Bess was polishing off her second eclair.

George watched her, an impatient look on her face.

"I'm coming, I'm coming," Bess told her cousin.

When the girls arrived at Beech Hill, Susan Caldwell was in her office.

"How's Henrik?" Nancy asked immediately.

Susan sighed. "Not very well, I'm afraid. He's regained consciousness, but he can't remember anything that happened."

Nancy knew that a blow to the head like the one he had received could cause short-term amnesia. It would probably clear up in a couple of days. Unfortunately, whatever Henrik van der Hune knew about the missing carving would remain a mystery for a while.

Nancy handed Susan the gray envelope with the provenance documents and explained what had happened at the Tidal Basin. Susan frowned. "That's odd. I wonder what that man was after." She flipped through the papers. "Everything here seems in order."

Then Nancy told her what John Riggs had said about the note and its contents.

"A death threat!" Susan paled.

Nancy nodded. "I spoke to Detective Briscoe," she went on. "He says the ink and the paper the thief used are pretty standard stuff—we'd never be able to trace them. But the handprint was made using mercuric sulfide. Riggs told us it's the same thing as cinnabar."

"Cinnabar!" Susan exclaimed. "Of course! That would explain the handprint's color."

"Where could someone get cinnabar?" Nancy asked the museum director.

Susan thought for a minute. "A while back we needed some for a display," she recalled. "We finally ordered it from a chemical warehouse. I think it was the only place around that carries it."

"Do you still have the company's number?" Nancy asked.

"I'll check my files. Hold on." Susan turned to

her filing cabinet and poked in a drawer. "Here it is." She pulled out the file and gave Nancy the supplier's name and number.

Nancy picked up the phone. "Let's find out if anyone in this area has ordered any lately," she said as she dialed.

After talking to several people at the warehouse, Nancy hung up the phone. On her face was a troubled expression.

"What's up?" asked George.

"They did get an order for mercuric sulfide," Nancy said. "A rush order—just last week."

"Who ordered it?" Susan asked.

"John Riggs," Nancy said.

A surprised silence fell over the room.

Susan swallowed hard.

"Riggs?" Bess repeated, confused. "But he told us he didn't have any."

Nancy gave her a meaningful look. "Exactly."

After discussing the case with Susan for a few more minutes, Nancy and her friends left Beech Hill and returned to the hotel. As they stepped off the elevator onto their floor, Nancy pulled out her electronic key card.

"Maybe after dinner we can go back to the Tidal Basin and show your dad the cherry blossoms," Bess suggested. "I bet they look gorgeous by sunset."

"That's a great idea," Nancy began. "He would . . ." She was about to slide the card into the door lock when her voice trailed off. The door to their room was already open.

"Don't go in there!" Bess cried, grabbing Nancy's arm.

Slowly, Nancy nudged the door open with her foot. "Hello?" she called.

There was no answer. She turned back to her friends. "Maybe it's the maid turning down the beds," she whispered.

Nancy pushed the door open all the way and stepped inside. She stifled her gasp. The covers of the bed were thrown off and the contents of the drawers were strewn across the floor.

Without saying a word, Nancy backed away. "Until we know for sure that the room is empty, we're not going in," she said firmly. She hurried back down the hall to where a hotel phone sat on a table. She dialed the security staff and reported the break-in.

Five minutes later the hotel security chief stepped off the elevator. He wore dark pants and a white shirt, and the walkie-talkie attached to his belt crackled with static.

"Ms. Drew?" He stepped toward Nancy. "You wait here. I'll check your room."

A few minutes later he poked his head out. "It's empty—come on in. I'd like you to let me know if anything's missing."

The girls quickly inspected the room and declared that nothing had been taken. "I'm sorry this happened," the security chief said. "I'll arrange to have a maid come to straighten up. And I'll take your key cards and have them recoded so the thief can't get in again." He hesitated. "Any chance you left the door open when you left earlier?" Nancy shook her head. "No," she said quietly.

The security chief shrugged. "Maybe the intruder somehow got hold of one of your cards and made a copy." He pointed to Nancy's expensive camera, which was sitting on the bureau. "It doesn't seem like a typical break-in. I'm surprised that's still here." Apologizing again, he left the room.

Nancy traded glances with Bess and George. "Maybe the intruder didn't care about valuable goods like cameras."

Bess picked up a pillow from the floor and tossed it on one of the beds. "He wanted the provenance documents we just returned to Beech Hill."

"My thoughts exactly." Nancy sighed.

George had been quiet as she cautiously surveyed the room. Suddenly she gasped. A scrap of paper rested on the carpet at her feet. Scrawled across it in menacing black letters were Mayan glyphs and a deep red handprint.

"Another note!" Nancy exclaimed. She knelt for a closer look. "Does anyone have a plastic bag?"

"Here." George pulled a plastic laundry bag from an empty bureau drawer.

Carefully, Nancy put the note in the bag. Then she went to the phone and called Detective Briscoe.

After filling in the detective, she dropped down on a bed. "He told me not to touch anything until he gets here."

"Do you suppose it's another death threat, Nancy?" Bess sounded frightened. "Aimed at *you* this time?"

Nancy crossed her arms. "Let's not jump to any conclusions," she said. "We'll take the note to John Riggs tomorrow and let *him* tell us what it says."

But underneath her calm exterior, Nancy couldn't help feeling spooked. Maybe Bess was right. Maybe this time the note *had* been written to her. And maybe its message was just as threatening.

The chambermaid arrived, and Nancy asked her to return in half an hour, after the police had arrived.

As she hesitated in the doorway, Detective Briscoe arrived with some men from the forensics lab and strode inside.

He took the new note from Nancy and glanced at it. "Stop by tomorrow and I'll give you the lab results on this one. We'll see if it matches the previous note."

"Can I have it back or get a copy?" she asked.

Briscoe shrugged. "Sure. But I wouldn't get my hopes up about tracking down the person who wrote it, Nancy," he said. "This case may never be solved. Art thefts are very hard to trace."

Nancy bit her lip as he shooed them out of the room. She didn't know what the note said or who had written it, but at least it was a clue. When would Detective Briscoe start taking this case more seriously? He might not believe they could find the thief, but she wasn't going to let him stop her.

Later, downstairs in the hotel restaurant, the girls ordered dinner. When Carson Drew joined them, he was frowning. "What happened? I ran into the police upstairs."

He listened carefully as they told him about their ransacked room. "The first note was for whoever discovered the carving was missing," he mused aloud. "But I'll bet this one was left specifically for you." He looked at his daughter, his eyes filled with concern. "My guess is that somebody out there wants you to stay out of this business. Whoever it is is serious." His next words hung in the air. "Dead serious."

In bed that night Nancy couldn't sleep. Mayan glyphs and symbols filled her head. Finally she dozed off, dreaming about a strange-looking plumed bird soaring above the Tidal Basin. It dipped down to peck at a terrifying black jaguar. They writhed together in a smoky haze as bells rang shrilly in the distance.

Suddenly Nancy awoke and realized the bell she'd heard in her dream was the phone beside her bed. She groped for the receiver.

"Hello," she murmured, still half asleep.

"Nancy Drew?" a softly accented voice whispered.

"Yes," she replied.

"Would you like to know more about Lord Pacal?"

Nancy sat straight up in bed. "Yes."

"Then ask John Riggs." With that, the line clicked dead.

7

A Suspicious Character

Nancy hung up the phone, trembling. Bess and George, roused by the phone's ringing, groggily asked Nancy what the call was about.

Quickly, she told them.

"Did you recognize the voice?" Bess asked.

Nancy shook her head. "It sounded like a man with a slight accent. But I couldn't really tell what kind of accent."

"Alejandro has an accent," Bess said.

"So does Henrik van der Hune," Nancy added. "But Susan Caldwell says he has no memory of the theft right now. I'd doubt he'd be calling."

"The caller told you to ask John Riggs about Lord Pacal," George mused. "Does that mean Riggs is the thief?"

"Could be. Or that's what the caller wants me to think," Nancy said. She stared at her friends. "One thing's for sure—John Riggs is looking more and more suspicious."

After breakfast the next morning, the girls hopped into the rental car and drove to Taylor Sinclair's gallery. It was located in a townhouse on a quiet side street just off Dupont Circle. As they pulled up, Nancy was surprised to see that it wasn't as well kept as the other nearby buildings. Taylor Sinclair had struck her as someone who cared a lot about how things looked.

They climbed the steep stairs to the gallery. Just inside the entrance a young man sat behind a modern steel and chrome desk. He looked up as they entered.

"Is Taylor Sinclair in?" Nancy asked.

The man raised his eyebrows. "May I tell him who's calling?"

Nancy gave him her name and watched as he retreated to an inner office.

While they waited, the girls took a quick look around the gallery. Several display cases artfully arranged in the stark white space held small, exquisitely carved objects, mostly in the same greenstone used in the Lord Pacal carving.

Bess drifted over to a case against one wall. "Hey," she called. "Look at this beautiful jewelry."

Before Nancy could reply, Taylor Sinclair entered the gallery space.

"Ms. Drew." He extended his hand. "You wanted to see me?"

Nancy shook his hand. "Would it be possible for me to speak with you in private?" she asked.

He nodded and then politely showed her into the back room. Bess and George stayed in the gallery.

The room held an enormous desk, surrounded by what Nancy assumed were pre-Columbian sculptures. Taylor seated himself in a black leather chair behind the desk and motioned for her to sit in the brown suede armchair across from him.

"What can I help you with?" he asked, his hands poised in front of him, fingertips pressed together.

Nancy got right to the point. "I saw you and Henrik van der Hune having a heated argument yesterday," she said. "He seemed very upset."

Sinclair rolled his eyes. "Henrik is like that," he replied.

"What do you mean?" Nancy asked.

"He gets too involved with the objects at Beech Hill," Sinclair explained. "I suppose most curators do, but he carries it to an extreme. They become like children to him. To me, art is to be admired, but it's also something that is bought and sold."

"Is that what you were arguing about?" Nancy inquired.

"In a way," Sinclair replied vaguely.

"Shortly after you argued, he was knocked down

by a falling statue in the garden," Nancy said. "He had to be taken to the hospital."

"Oh, no!" Sinclair sat forward on his chair. "I drove off rather miffed after I talked to him, but I—" He stopped and cleared his throat. "Was he badly hurt?"

"He has temporary amnesia," Nancy reported.

Sinclair sighed. "What a shame."

Nancy asked him a few more questions about the sale of the Mayan carving to Beech Hill, but she couldn't get any new information out of him. Then she asked him about John Riggs. "Is it true he was trying to buy Lord Pacal, too?" she asked.

"Oh, yes, I guess he did make a bid," Sinclair said with a disdainful sniff. "A ridiculously low bid, as I recall."

"Was he bitter about losing the bidding war?" Nancy pressed.

Sinclair shrugged. "Not that I could tell," he replied. "He and I are still on good terms. The art world is very small, you know. It doesn't do to make enemies."

Just then Sinclair's assistant buzzed him to announce a phone call. Sinclair excused himself, and Nancy said goodbye and left his office.

In the gallery, she gestured for Bess and George to follow her downstairs.

"That was useless," Nancy complained as they reached the sidewalk. "Sinclair told me he was mad at Henrik van der Hune before the accident, but he wouldn't say why. He just said he drove off in a huff after they spoke."

George gave her an odd look. "Sinclair said he drove off *before* van der Hune entered the garden?"

Nancy nodded. "Yes. I did see him get into his car," she recalled.

George stopped in the middle of the sidewalk. "Well, I saw him in the garden right before I heard you scream," she declared. "Remember, Bess?"

Bess nodded. "He was walking down the path that led to the entrance," she confirmed.

"Why would Taylor Sinclair lie?" Nancy wondered. She frowned, her mind working to put this new piece of the puzzle in place. "I was beginning to think that I was wrong, that the falling statue was just a freak accident. But now . . ."

"Maybe Henrik van der Hune would be able to tell you more about the conversation between him and Sinclair," George suggested.

"If only he had his memory," Nancy said, finishing the thought. She hopped into the car. "Let's head over to Beech Hill and talk to Susan Caldwell again. Maybe she can shed more light on this situation."

At Beech Hill Susan listened thoughtfully to Nancy's story about the break-in. Nancy also told her about the new note and the phone call in the middle of the night.

"Now that we know John Riggs ordered some

cinnabar, he looks very suspicious," Nancy concluded.

The museum director sighed. "He's always been jealous of some of the things we have in our collection," she admitted. "I know he desperately wanted Lord Pacal for his museum. But I can't believe he'd actually steal it. He'd risk ruining his reputation in the museum world—not to mention spending time in jail." She paused. "Are you going to let him look at this new note?"

Nancy nodded. "Briscoe is going to give me a copy, and I'll show it to Riggs this afternoon," she said. "There's just one other thing troubling me I want to ask you about."

She explained how she had seen Taylor Sinclair arguing with Henrik van der Hune. Sinclair had said he'd driven away, Nancy added, but George had seen him in the garden just before van der Hune's accident.

Susan frowned. "I was going to visit Henrik right after lunch," she said. "Maybe you girls should come with me and try to get his side of the story, that is, if he remembers anything yet."

Nancy suggested that Bess and George go to the hospital while she went to the police station to pick up the lab report on the note and the copy of it.

They ate a quick lunch in the gardens, then Susan drove off to the hospital with Bess and George. They agreed to meet up later at the Museum of Natural History, where John Riggs worked.

Nancy walked to the rental car and then headed for the Georgetown police department. Detective Briscoe was sipping coffee from a Styrofoam cup when she knocked on the door to his office.

"Have you analyzed the note?" she asked.

Briscoe nodded. "Same paper and ink and cinnabar as the other one," he said. "And we found some fingerprints."

"Yes?" Nancy said hopefully.

"Couldn't identify them," he said. "The only prints we have on file are of people who've been in trouble with the law. Your intruder must have a clean record."

Nancy nodded, feeling let down. "Our expert on Mayan glyphs says the first note contained a death threat."

Briscoe looked surprised. "Maybe this one's a threat, too, from someone who doesn't want you involved in this case," he said.

"It may be the same person who interpreted it for me." Nancy told him that John Riggs had recently bought cinnabar from a chemical warehouse.

"But it's not unusual that he'd have some of this, is it?" replied the detective. "After all, he studies this stuff."

"He does," Nancy agreed. "But he told us he didn't have any."

Briscoe's eyebrows raised. "Might be worth following up," he said.

"That's what I'd like to do," Nancy told him.

"Can you photocopy the note for your files and then let me show him the original?"

Briscoe nodded and led her to the copier. "Let me know what you find out," he said as the machine copied the note. "I have to say, when Susan Caldwell told me you were a detective I didn't expect much. But I'm impressed."

Nancy took the note back with a friendly grin. At last Detective Briscoe was treating her like a real detective.

Nancy left the police station and drove to the Museum of Natural History, determined to have another talk with John Riggs. Finding her way upstairs, she knocked lightly on Riggs's half-opened door.

"Come in," he called. When she pushed it open, he looked up from his computer. "Oh," he said. "I wasn't expecting you."

"I'm sorry to stop by without an appointment," Nancy began. "But there's something I need to show you." She handed him the second note.

"Where did this show up?" he asked.

Nancy watched him carefully as she told him that her hotel room had been broken into. The expression on his face barely changed. Actually, he seemed more interested in the glyphs than in her story.

"This is very similar to the other one," he said, squinting at the page. Then he raised his eyes and looked at her directly. "Whoever left this note

71

wants you to stop looking for the carving," he said. "It says your skin will be flayed and your intestines pulled out if you continue the investigation."

A chill ran up Nancy's spine. "Oh, is that all?" she commented drily.

"The curses are taken from ancient Mayan rituals," John Riggs said. "I'm sure they're not to be taken literally. But you get the message."

Nancy was about to bring the conversation around to the order of cinnabar when Riggs's phone rang. He spoke softly for a couple minutes, scribbling on his desk note pad. Nancy glanced sideways toward the address and time he was writing down.

Riggs put his hand over the mouthpiece. "I'm sorry," he said. "I'm really rather busy. Is there anything else?"

"I'm afraid there is," Nancy said firmly. She wasn't about to let him dismiss her before she'd even gotten to the point of her visit.

Riggs frowned. "Then let me finish this call—in private." He tapped the desk impatiently with the eraser end of his pencil. "Can you come back in ten minutes?"

There was nothing Nancy could do but agree to leave. She wandered aimlessly down the hallway that connected the offices to the outer gallery. Who was Riggs talking to? she wondered.

Someone brushed past her in the narrow corridor, murmuring an apology. Something made Nancy turn and look at him, but all she saw was the back of a slight, dark-haired figure heading down the hall.

She went out to the gallery and halfheartedly began to examine the contents of one of the display cases.

The ten minutes I have to kill before returning to John Riggs's office is going to seem like ten hours, she thought impatiently. Besides, now I'm going to be late to meet Bess and George.

"Nancy!"

As if on cue, Bess and George hurried toward her. They looked flustered and out of breath.

"I just saw him!" George exclaimed. "We were waiting for you in the lobby, as we agreed, and we saw him come in. We followed him up here, but then we lost him."

"Who?" Nancy asked. "What are you talking about?"

"The man who tried to run you over at the Tidal Basin," Bess blurted out.

Nancy glanced around. There were no other people in the gallery except for a group of French tourists. Where could he have gone?

Then something clicked in Nancy's mind. Her hand went up to her mouth. Now she knew why she had turned to look back at that man who'd bumped her.

"I saw him, too!" she exclaimed. "And he was heading straight for John Riggs's office!"

8

A Strange Gathering

The girls wheeled around and raced toward the hallway that led to the offices.

It was empty. John Riggs's office was empty, too. Nancy gazed around the room in disappointment. The director's desk chair was pushed away from the desk, and his computer was still on.

"He obviously left in a hurry," Nancy said, "which is strange because he told me to meet him back here in ten minutes."

"Did he leave because of the phone call? Or because of the man we saw?" Bess asked.

Nancy shrugged. "I don't know. What bothers me is that both of them left without our seeing them. There must be another way out besides the main doors."

Nancy walked up and down the hallway. Sure enough, after a sharp turn, the hall led to another gallery with a side exit.

The girls returned to Riggs's office. Inside the room Nancy paused, thinking.

"I know that look on your face, Nancy Drew," George warned. "You're about to do something you probably shouldn't."

Nancy nodded. "Before I left, he took some notes on this pad," she said. She looked at the pad and saw that the top sheet had been torn off. She picked up a pencil.

"Nancy, aren't you trespassing?" George asked her uneasily.

"He did ask me to return," Nancy said, defending herself. She rubbed the side of the pencil point over the pad. Soon an impression of what Riggs had scribbled on the top sheet formed on the pad. It was an address in suburban Maryland, and below that was written, "7 P.M. tonight." Carefully, Nancy tore off the piece of paper and stuffed it into her jeans pocket.

Bess was standing by a long table behind Riggs's desk. She picked up a small glass bottle and examined it closely.

"Nancy!" she exclaimed a second later. "Look!" She passed the bottle to her friend.

Nancy took the bottle. As she peered inside, she inhaled sharply. The bottle contained bloodred powder. A label on the bottle bore the name of the chemical supplier she'd called the day before. Underneath the supplier's name were typed the words *mercuric sulfide.*

"Cinnabar!" George breathed excitedly.

"Look at this!" Bess pointed to a pad of artist's paper, a bottle of black ink, and some brushes, all lying on the table.

The three girls looked at one another, aware of what this discovery might mean.

Nancy tore another sheet of paper from Riggs's desk pad. Tipping the bottle of cinnabar over the paper, she poured out a small amount, folded it up into a little packet and placed it in her pocket.

"We'll have Briscoe's lab test this," she told her friends. "Now let's make sure that everything's put back just as we found it. We don't want Riggs to know we were snooping." They quickly straightened up the office and left.

As they walked to their car, Bess and George told Nancy about their visit to Henrik van der Hune.

"He still doesn't remember anything from the day he was hurt," said George.

"And the doctors can't tell us when his memory will improve. It could be tomorrow; it could be weeks," Bess added.

Nancy sighed. Did Henrik van der Hune hold the key to this mystery?

"Well, we can't wait for him to clear up this mystery for us," Nancy declared. "Let's grab a quick dinner. I believe we've got a date with Mr. Riggs tonight at seven."

At a nearby pizzeria the girls split a large pie and pored over a local road map. At twilight they found themselves on River Road, following the Potomac River upstream into Maryland.

"Turn here," directed Bess from the passenger seat, where she was holding the map. Nancy made a left turn onto a heavily wooded street.

George looked out the window, straining her eyes to read the numbers on the houses. All the homes were large and set far back from the road.

"It must be the next one," George informed Nancy. "Wow. Look at all these cars."

As Nancy parked at the side of the road, she noticed they weren't the only ones paying a visit to this particular address that night. It was only a quarter to seven, and both sides of the road were lined with cars.

This wasn't at all what Nancy had expected. She'd thought Riggs was paying a private visit. From all the cars, though, she guessed he was attending a party.

"Let's see if we can find someplace to watch what's going on," she told her friends. They left the car, making sure no one saw them, and walked up the road to the house. To the left of the front door they spotted the perfect hiding place—a clump of shrubs. The girls hurried across the lawn and crouched beneath the bushes.

From their hiding place they could easily watch the front door. Soon an older woman dressed in dark pants and a matching jacket walked up to the door and was let into the house. As the front door opened, Nancy peered into the front hall. The woman stepped inside, stopping to pick up what looked like a folded burlap robe from a small table. She pulled it over her head, then donned an odd, feathered mask. Abruptly the door closed behind her.

"That's so weird," George whispered. "Is this a costume party—or what?"

"Who knows?" Nancy mumbled back to her friend.

As the girls watched, each person who entered did the same thing. For some reason the feathered masks reminded Nancy of her weird dream the night before. What kind of party was this?

She reached into her jeans and pulled out a small notepad. "I'll stay here and watch the door. Why don't you two take this pad and pencil and write down all the license plate numbers of the cars parked out front. Tomorrow we can have Briscoe do a computer search to identify the cars' owners."

"Okay," George agreed. "Will you be all right alone for a few minutes?"

"Sure," Nancy told her.

The two cousins inched out from behind the

shrubs and headed for the street. A few minutes later two more guests entered. As she watched them go in, Nancy realized she could easily slip inside and get a better idea of what was happening.

She waited until the guests were safely inside, then she hopped out of the bushes and strolled up to the front door.

After she rang the doorbell, a middle-aged man in a tweed jacket opened the door. He waved Nancy toward the table where the rough cloth robes and feathered masks lay. Nancy quickly slipped a robe over her hooded sweatshirt and dark jeans, then put on a mask.

In the living room a crowd of people milled about, chatting. The room was almost bare of furniture, and the only light came from candles, giving off incense-scented smoke. On one side of the room an enormous plate-glass window looked out over the Potomac River. In front of the window sat a small table, which reminded Nancy of an altar. The silvery light from a full moon fell across the masked figures gathered in the room.

Suddenly the room went silent. Nancy heard primitive-sounding drums and a strange flutelike refrain. As she watched, all heads turned toward an arched doorway. A procession of robed participants, some with ornately painted faces, marched single file into the room. They were all beating on skin-covered drums or playing clay pipes.

Bringing up the rear was a tall man in a feathered

costume. His intricately beaded headpiece completely covered his face and head. In front of him he carried an enormous, patterned pottery vessel.

The procession cut through the middle of the room, heading toward the altar by the window. As the feathered man reached the altar, he held the vessel up above his head. His sleeves fell back, and Nancy noticed his skinny forearms were covered with freckles.

As the music grew louder, the people in the room began to chant. Nancy's mask slipped for a moment as she tried to join the chant, and her fingers fumbled as she tried to put it back in place. The masked man next to her turned and looked straight at her when her mask fell. For all I know, she thought nervously, he could be John Riggs.

The chanting continued as trays of large goblets were brought up to the altar. The feathered man began to scoop a liquid from the larger vessel into each cup, then passed them out.

Suddenly a cup appeared in front of Nancy. It was held by a cloaked figure wearing an intricately carved greenstone ring on one finger.

Nancy took the cup and pretended to drink, knowing it was never smart to drink an unidentified liquid. But as she raised the cup to her lips, the man next to her turned abruptly, knocking her arm hard with his elbow. The drink splashed into Nancy's mouth before she could do anything to stop it. It

80

tasted like nothing more than heavily sweetened hot chocolate—she hoped that was what it was.

Nancy suddenly remembered that her sweatshirt had a pouch in front. She discreetly reached into the neck of the robe and tucked the goblet into the pouch. Maybe she could get Briscoe to figure out what the liquid was.

The chanting continued, and so did the steady drumbeat. Nancy felt herself swaying in rhythm to the music as the room grew hotter and smokier. A man in spotted fur began to dance, looking like a half-man, half-jaguar.

Then, as Nancy gazed around the room at the flickering candles, the tiny lights began to swirl around and around. She felt her legs buckle, then give way. A hand reached out to stop her. On one finger was a familiar ring. Greenstone, she thought.

Then everything went black.

9

Trapped!

The next thing Nancy knew, she was lying in the dark on a cold cement floor. She tried to move her arms, but her hands seemed to be bound behind her. A cloth had been tied around her head to gag her mouth.

How had she gotten here? She remembered accidentally drinking the strange potion at the ceremony, then getting caught up in the chanting and dancing.

I must have passed out, she realized. What was in that cup?

As she tried to wriggle free, the rope binding her hands bit into her wrists. Across the room, she could make out a thin line of dim light. A door. She inched steadily toward it, then her foot struck something hard. A rake clattered to the ground, its metal tines narrowly missing her head.

Was it her imagination, or did she hear arguing voices beyond the door? She opened her mouth to yell for help, but the gag was firmly in place.

"I say leave her here!" a muffled, angry voice commanded. The voice sounded vaguely familiar, but in her groggy state Nancy couldn't place it. Then the arguing stopped, and around her it was completely quiet again.

As her eyes got used to the darkness, she began to scan the room. There was a workbench scattered with trowels and flowerpots, and several gardening tools hung from the walls.

I must be in a garden shed, she thought.

The door rattled loudly, jarring Nancy. Someone was trying to break in, but was it someone trying to help her or her abductor coming back to harm her?

Nancy squirmed as far away from the door as she could.

With a crash, the door swung open. Moonlight streamed in, silhouetting a dark figure. She couldn't see who it was, but from his build, she knew it was a man.

Nancy watched in horror as the man picked up a shovel, hoisted it above his head, and moved toward her. She stiffened and closed her eyes as he began to bring it down on her.

Then, suddenly, the shovel clattered to the ground and her attacker collapsed. Another man had tackled him, and now the two were rolling in the doorway, grappling fiercely.

Nancy caught a quick glimpse of a face. Alejandro del Rio! But it was so dark, she wasn't sure of anything. Was he the one who had tried to attack her? Or the one coming to her rescue?

Finally one man broke free and dashed for the open door. Slowly the other man rose to his feet. Nancy pulled back as he bent over her. It was Alejandro.

"I won't hurt you," he whispered. "I'm on your side. Let me untie your hands."

Not knowing what else to do, Nancy let him remove the gag and begin to loosen the ropes. Outside she heard feet pounding across the grass. Bess and George burst into the shed.

"We heard fighting," George said, panting hard. "We were looking for you on the grounds when . . ." Her voice trailed off as she saw Nancy's bound hands. "Oh, my gosh. Who did this to you?"

Alejandro looked up, and George sprang forward to push him away from Nancy.

"It's okay, George," Nancy croaked. "He saved me."

George looked from Nancy to Alejandro with a confused expression. "Are you sure?"

Still feeling groggy, Nancy nodded slowly.

Alejandro continued to work on the rope around Nancy's hands. "We'd better get out of here as soon as we can," he said calmly. "Before anyone else comes back to see about the prisoner."

"We saw a man running from the shed," Bess said. "It's dark out, but I'm pretty sure it was the man who attacked you at the Tidal Basin."

Alejandro turned to Nancy with an odd look on his face. "He attacked you at the Tidal Basin?"

Nancy nodded and sat up. "He wasn't just asking you for change, was he?" she asked Alejandro.

Alejandro helped Nancy to her feet and motioned for George to hold her up on the other side. His face was dark with emotion. "Let's get her to the car," he suggested in a tight voice. He turned to Nancy. "I'll tell you all I know, but not until a doctor has taken a good look at you."

Nancy tried to stand, but her legs wobbled like jelly. Together, Alejandro and the two girls helped Nancy across the lawn and over to the rental car. It was now one of the few cars left on the street. How much time had passed while she was in the shed?

Alejandro helped her into the backseat. "I'll drive my car back downtown," he said. "Tell me where you're staying and your room number, and I'll meet you there."

Nancy looked at him. Just hours ago she never would have believed him, but tonight he had saved her life. She quickly gave him the information he wanted.

On the drive back to Washington, Bess and

George told Nancy what had gone on after she entered the house.

"When we got back to the shrubs after writing down those license plate numbers, you weren't there," George said, negotiating a winding turn on River Road. "It had gotten quiet outside. We figured you'd gone in, so we just waited."

"An hour or so passed, and then everyone poured out the front door in street clothes," Bess continued. "When you didn't appear, we started to get worried."

George broke in. "A little while later we heard the fighting and followed the sounds."

"Nancy, what went on in the house?" Bess asked.

Nancy leaned her head against the back of her seat. "It was so strange!" Slowly, she told her friends what she could remember about the ceremony. The pounding drums and primitive chanting. The man dressed as a jaguar. The feathered costumes. And the strange potion. It was obvious to her now that she'd been drugged. But by whom?

As she mentioned drinking the potion, she remembered that she'd taken the cup. She reached into her sweatshirt pocket. To her surprise the cup was still there and in one piece.

When they pulled up to the hotel, Bess hopped out and helped Nancy up the steps and into the lobby while George parked the car. Then Bess arranged for the hotel doctor to come up to their room.

Upstairs, Bess persuaded Nancy to lie down until the doctor came. Then she knocked on Carson Drew's door to tell him what had happened.

Carson Drew hurried into the girls' room. "Nancy! Are you all right?" he cried, looking very worried.

"I'm fine, Dad," Nancy reassured him. "Just tired and a little dizzy."

When the hotel doctor arrived, he checked Nancy's vital signs and shone a light in her eyes. In a halting voice Nancy explained what had happened to her. Then she handed the goblet to the doctor and told him the drink had tasted like heavily sweetened hot chocolate.

He put the cup up to his nose and inhaled. "It smells like hot chocolate," he said, setting the cup on the night table by Nancy's bed. "But I suspect it was laced with a strong sedative, based on your reaction and the look of your eyes."

He closed up his bag. "Get a good night's rest," he told her. "You should be fine in the morning. Perhaps just a bit sluggish."

After the doctor left, Nancy and her friends told Carson Drew more about the event-filled evening. Nancy was yawning sleepily when a soft knock came on the door.

"I'll get it." Carson Drew sprung up. It was Alejandro.

After asking about Nancy's health, Alejandro seated himself in a chair near the bed. "I suppose

87

you want to know what my connection is to this," he said rather sheepishly.

They all nodded.

"I have to admit that at first I didn't trust you," he said to Nancy. "I wasn't sure I wanted Lord Pacal to be returned to Beech Hill. After all, I thought he shouldn't have been there in the first place. But after what happened tonight," he went on, "I'm convinced we have to band together if we're going to find him."

Nancy spoke up. "I understand how you feel about Lord Pacal, Alejandro."

"Then you should also understand that I'm no thief. I think stealing is wrong," he replied.

Nancy looked him in the eyes. "What *was* going on at that house tonight?" she asked softly.

"I was there to meet someone," he confessed.

"Who?" Nancy pressed.

"The man who tried to hurt you in the shed. The same man who attacked you at the Tidal Basin."

"But why?" Carson Drew demanded. "What does he want from my daughter?"

Alejandro took a deep breath. "He asked me to meet him there. He said he had information to give me about the theft of Lord Pacal."

"What's his name?" Nancy asked eagerly. Maybe they were close at last to finding the thief.

"His name is Ricardo Martinez," Alejandro answered. "And he's one of the most notorious art smugglers in Mexico."

10

A Not-So-Secret Society

"An art smuggler!" Nancy sat right up.

"Well known in pre-Columbian circles," Alejandro added. "Martinez is not a nice fellow. But he's very good at avoiding the authorities."

"Why did he contact you?" George asked.

"The first time he called was the morning after the theft of Lord Pacal," Alejandro explained. "He called me at the consulate and said he had some information about the theft he wanted to share. That's why I went to John Riggs's office the other day—to ask him what he knew about Martinez. I've met Riggs on a number of occasions, and he knows everyone in the pre-Columbian art world. I figured he'd know Martinez."

Nancy suddenly remembered seeing Martinez in

the hallway outside Riggs's office, but she didn't stop Alejandro to tell him that.

"When I saw you at Riggs's office, I panicked," Alejandro admitted. "I didn't want you to think I was involved with the theft. Especially since my opinions had already made me a suspect," he added with a wry grin.

"Your running away didn't exactly help your cause," Nancy told him.

Alejandro gave a nervous laugh. "Of course, I know that now," he said. "But I'm a diplomat, not a criminal. I'm not sure how to behave when I'm under suspicion."

Everyone in the room smiled at the young Mexican.

"As you know, I met Ricardo at the Tidal Basin," Alejandro went on. "He had just told me that someone I knew well was the thief. He hadn't told me that name yet. Then he spotted you following me, Nancy. Apparently, he'd been tipped off that you were looking for Lord Pacal. So he refused to talk to me any further."

"After you left, Martinez ran me into the Tidal Basin with his bike," Nancy told Alejandro. "But I think what he really wanted was the envelope I was carrying. It had the provenance documents in it."

Alejandro raised his eyebrows. "How would he know what was in the envelope? And why would he want the provenance documents?"

"I don't know," Nancy admitted. "Did he tell

you why he wanted to meet you at the house in Maryland?"

"He said the thief himself would be there," Alejandro said. "And he would point him out to me."

Nancy's eyes widened. "Why was he willing to do that?"

Alejandro shrugged. "I don't know. Maybe he'd been double-crossed somehow. Maybe he just didn't like this person."

"Whom did he point out?" Nancy asked eagerly.

Alejandro shook his head. "When I got there at nine, the house was deserted," he said. "I walked around the property. That's when I noticed Martinez outside the shed, arguing with a man in a robe."

"Could you tell who that was?" Nancy asked.

Alejandro shook his head. "I was too far away."

Nancy began to tell Alejandro what she knew. She mentioned the cinnabar, ink, and paper they'd discovered that afternoon in John Riggs's office.

Alejandro's face showed his shock. "I can't imagine John Riggs having anything to do with the theft of Lord Pacal," he declared.

"He wanted it badly for his museum," Nancy reminded him.

"But what could he possibly do with it if he stole it?" Alejandro asked. "He couldn't very well put it on display afterward."

"He was invited to that house," Nancy told him.

91

She explained how she'd found the address on Riggs's notepad. "You know John Riggs, and Martinez told you that Lord Pacal's thief was someone you know."

"I know many people in the pre-Columbian art world," Alejandro pointed out.

Suddenly, he noticed the cup sitting on the nightstand next to Nancy's bed.

"Where did you get that goblet?" he asked.

"At the ceremony in the house," Nancy replied. She quickly described the events of that evening.

Alejandro looked astonished. "It sounds like the ceremony of the Vision Serpent," he said. "It's one of the most ancient Mayan rituals. The Maya believed it summoned visions from the world of the spirits." He reached for the cup and examined it closely.

For the first time, as Alejandro held it, Nancy noticed the Mayan glyphs that decorated the cup. What do they mean? she wondered.

Alejandro looked baffled. "I don't get it. Why would they be performing the Mayan ritual in that house?"

"That's something you'll have to find out tomorrow," Carson Drew said firmly. "Nancy, you look exhausted. I think it's time for this particular evening to come to a close."

"Okay, Dad," Nancy agreed. Before Alejandro left, she promised to keep him informed of any new developments in the case.

"And I'll let you know if Martinez contacts me again," Alejandro said. "Although after what happened tonight, I seriously doubt he will."

Alejandro and Carson Drew said good night and left, and the girls settled down for the night. Nancy's last thought before her head hit the pillow was that it was time to confront John Riggs with the evidence that linked him to the theft of Lord Pacal.

After a quick breakfast the next morning, Nancy, Bess, and George headed over to the Georgetown police department. Carson Drew had made his daughter promise that the police station would be her first stop of the day. He wanted her to fill in the police on everything that had happened the night before.

Detective Briscoe invited the girls into his office. Nancy told him about the party and what she and her friends had found in John Riggs's office.

"I thought Riggs was the one who said he didn't have any cinnabar," Briscoe said.

Nancy nodded. "Obviously he lied." She pulled out the scrap of folded paper that contained the red powder. "Can your lab analyze this?"

Briscoe carefully took it from her. "I'll get it down there this morning."

"So is the name Ricardo Martinez familiar to you?" George asked the detective. "We think he's the guy who's been trying to stop Nancy."

"I've heard that name before," Briscoe told her.

"Several people in international art circles have mentioned him. I'll try to track him down. Maybe after last night we can pin an assault charge on him."

Nancy nodded. "That's what I was thinking." She handed him the list of license plate numbers. "Here's a guest list from last night's party."

Briscoe glanced at the list. "We'll trace these plates."

"This may also be a lead." Nancy pulled the goblet out of her bag. "My drink was served in this cup. I'm pretty sure I was the only one at the ceremony who was drugged."

Briscoe turned the goblet over in his hands. "It looks like there's enough residue in here to test," he said. "I'll send it to the lab."

"Uh, do you think I could have it back?" Nancy asked. "Just for a couple of hours?"

Briscoe raised his eyebrows. "Why?"

"I'd like to show it to John Riggs and ask him to interpret the glyphs. I also think that showing him the cup might jar him into a confession."

Briscoe hesitated. "So far, the only evidence we have against Riggs is circumstantial. We'll need more proof if we want to prove he's guilty. I—"

"Does that mean it's okay with you?" Nancy interrupted hastily.

Briscoe grinned and nodded. "I have a feeling I couldn't stop you even if I tried."

Bess and George laughed while Nancy blushed

94

and tried to look indignant. "Now, what makes you say that?"

"Just a hunch," the detective told her lightly. Then he handed her the cup and promised his lab would go right to work on the cinnabar sample.

In front of the station house, George turned to Nancy. "To the museum?" she asked. "To confront Riggs?"

Nancy shook her head. "No, I want to go to Maryland first."

"We're not going back to that house, are we?" Bess stared at her friend.

"How else will I find out what was going on there last night?" Nancy asked.

Bess sighed as she climbed in the car. "I just hope no one's trying to summon visions from the world of spirits again," she muttered.

Me, too, Nancy added silently as she started up the car and headed toward the suburbs.

In the light of day, the site of the previous night's party seemed completely ordinary. When Nancy rang the doorbell of the large Tudor-style house, a pleasant-looking middle-aged woman answered.

Nancy quickly introduced herself and her friends.

"We were here last night," she went on, "and I'm pretty sure I left my jacket. May we come in and look for it?"

The woman looked uncertain but let them in.

Nancy stepped into the hall and caught a quick glimpse of the living room. For a moment she almost doubted her memory. Today the large room was filled with furniture and sunlight streamed in through the windows. Was I really here last night? she thought. Did that really happen to me?

But the woman confirmed Nancy wasn't just imagining things. While she rummaged in her coat closet, looking for Nancy's nonexistent jacket, she chatted away. "Wasn't that a wonderful ceremony last night?"

"Yes," Nancy replied cautiously. "Very authentic."

"It really is the highlight of the Pre-Columbian Society's year," the woman added.

The girls traded glances behind the woman's back. The Pre-Columbian Society? Was that some sort of art collectors' group? Or a Mayan cult?

The woman looked at Nancy. "I don't think I know you," she said. "Are you a new member?"

Nancy thought fast. "Actually, I came with a new member. He wants me to join."

The woman raised her eyebrows. "Oh, really? Now, who's—"

"There it is," George interrupted her abruptly. "Nancy, isn't that your jacket?" She pulled out a tweed blazer.

"No," Nancy replied, after pretending to examine it. "It looks like mine, but it's not."

She turned to the woman. "By the way, what was

96

that beverage we drank last night? It was awfully good."

"Oh, that." The woman laughed. "Hot cocoa mix. Straight out of the box. It's not authentic, but it is quick." She pushed aside the last coat hanger. "I'm sorry, but I don't think your jacket is here."

"Oh, well." Nancy acted disappointed. "I must have left it somewhere else. Thank you very much."

"No problem." The woman showed them to the door. "If you decide to join, just call Mr. Riggs."

"John Riggs?" Nancy's jaw nearly dropped.

"Yes," the woman said, not seeming to notice. "He's in charge of new memberships. He also led the ritual last night. He really does a terrific job."

"Yes, he sure does," Nancy agreed. She pushed Bess and George out the door before the dumbstruck looks on their faces gave them all away.

Back outside, Nancy strode purposefully toward the car.

"Did you hear that?" Bess said. "Riggs is in charge of new members for this society." George nodded grimly.

Nancy didn't say anything for a few minutes. Her mind was fixed on the memory of the feathered man at the altar. She remembered his holding up the large vessel and the sleeves of his robe falling away to reveal freckled arms. Of course that must have been John Riggs. Why hadn't she realized that before?

Nancy climbed into the car and turned to her

97

friends. "Guess who was also pouring those drinks last night?"

George gulped. "John Riggs?"

"I'd say that makes him suspect number one in the who-spiked-the-drink category," Nancy added. "Wouldn't you?"

11

The Missing Papers

John Riggs was in his office when the girls arrived. Nancy immediately pulled the cup out of her bag and placed it on his desk. "Can you tell me where this came from?" she asked.

He looked startled but picked up his glasses and examined the goblet carefully. "It's Mexican pottery," he said. "Cheap and mass produced."

"Do the glyphs mean anything?"

He shook his head. "They're just decorative." He handed the goblet back to Nancy. "Did you think it was antique?"

"No." Nancy said. "I was given a drink in it last night at a ceremony I attended out in Maryland." She paused. "I believe you were there."

Riggs shifted in his chair. "What makes you think that?" he asked.

"I saw you," Nancy replied matter-of-factly.

"And why were you there?" he asked, his face showing no emotion.

"Research." Nancy stared at him, waiting for him to say more.

"I guess you caught me," he said with a sigh. "Yes, I was at the house."

"What do you mean, I caught you?" Nancy asked. Was Riggs going to confess this easily?

"I don't like it to be known that I lead those ceremonies for the society," he said. She watched as his freckled face turned red. "It's a group of amateurs—ordinary people interested in the Maya. Scholars and serious art collectors think it's silly, but I enjoy it," he added defensively.

Nancy glanced at the table behind John Riggs's desk. He sounded sincere, but what about the other evidence that seemed to implicate him? The brushes, ink, and cinnabar still sat on the table. She gestured toward the bottle. "I thought you said you had no cinnabar," she said.

"Huh?" Riggs looked over his shoulder at the table. "Oh, those things. They just showed up the other day. I thought maybe a student had borrowed them and was finally returning them."

Nancy strolled over to the table and picked up the bottle. "The chemical house that sells this stuff says you ordered some last month," she said.

"What!" Riggs stared at her with an astonished expression. "I didn't order cinnabar."

"My guess is that these materials are what's been used to write the notes I've been showing you," Nancy went on.

Riggs gave her a panicked look. "Are you saying that I wrote them?"

"I'm not saying anything," Nancy replied evenly.

John Riggs rose from his desk. "I didn't write those notes."

"Then you probably won't mind if I take a sample of this cinnabar to the police detective investigating the theft of Lord Pacal." She poured some out onto a scrap of paper, just as she had the other day. She was hoping to provoke some kind of a reaction from Riggs. "His lab can analyze it and find out whether it was used to make the notes."

Riggs shrugged. "Fine. The police can test all they want. But I want you—and the police—to know I had nothing to do with the theft."

Nancy studied his face as he spoke. "The police are conducting a thorough investigation. I'm sure they'll get to the bottom of this." Then she scooped up the goblet and the cinnabar sample and left the office. Bess and George hurried after her.

"What do you think, Nan?" George asked once they were down the corridor. "Is he guilty?"

Nancy sighed. "I'm not sure," she answered truthfully. "He doesn't strike me as a liar." She stood lost in her thoughts for a moment. "I'd like to visit Henrik van der Hune next," she told her friends. "Somehow I think he holds the key to this mystery."

Henrik van der Hune was sitting up in bed when they arrived at the hospital. As Nancy and her friends entered his room, he reached for his thick glasses and put them on.

He still looks confused, Nancy thought with a sinking heart. He's not going to remember anything.

"Do I know you?" he asked in his thick accent.

Nancy approached his bed and stood next to him quietly. "I'm Susan Caldwell's friend Nancy Drew," she said. "I met you the day you were hurt. In fact, I was there when the statue fell."

He nodded. "Yes. Susan told me a young lady was with me."

"Mr. van der Hune," Nancy began, "I saw you at the Mexican consulate the morning of the accident. Do you remember why you were there?"

He frowned. "I'm afraid I still don't remember much of that day or the days before it. The doctors say I should get my memory back. I wish they could say when."

"Then you don't remember arguing with Taylor Sinclair?" Nancy probed. "I saw you two exchange some fairly heated words that morning."

Van der Hune squinted, trying to remember.

102

"Taylor . . . ," he mumbled. "I remember something about bad business. . . ."

"What kind of bad business?" Nancy asked.

Van der Hune sighed. "It's all such a blur in my mind. So frustrating . . ." His voice trailed off.

"Mr. van der Hune, I'm trying to help Susan find out how the Lord Pacal carving was stolen," Nancy pleaded. "Can you remember anything that could help me? Anything at all?"

The older man leaned back on his pillows and closed his eyes for a moment. He said nothing.

"You were carrying the provenance documents when you were hit by the falling statue. Did you have them for a reason?" Nancy asked.

Van der Hune's eyes fluttered open. "The provenance documents," he murmured. "Something in them . . . wasn't right."

"Wasn't right?" Nancy echoed.

He sighed again. "That's all I can tell you. The answer must be there, with the papers."

Nancy stood. She'd gotten all she could from the museum curator. She apologized for disturbing him, and the girls left.

"Poor Henrik," she remarked on the way out of the hospital. "He'll eventually get his memory back, but it must be frustrating."

"For him and us," George put in.

"Where next?" Bess asked.

"Beech Hill," Nancy replied. "Let's take another look at those provenance documents."

At Beech Hill Nancy told Susan Caldwell about her visit with Henrik van der Hune, as well as about the ceremony the night before.

When Nancy mentioned being drugged and abducted, Susan's mouth dropped open. "Oh, Nancy," she murmured. "When I asked for your help, I had no idea something like this would happen."

"I'm fine now," Nancy reassured her. "Just more determined than ever to figure out what's going on. Do you know anything about the Pre-Columbian Society?"

"Oh, that." Susan waved her hand dismissively. "I went to one of their rituals once." She shook her head. "Pretty amateur stuff. I have trouble understanding why Riggs would associate with them."

Nancy could see why John Riggs might want to conceal his involvement with the group. Susan clearly didn't think much of them.

"The society is a well-meaning group of people with a genuine interest in Mayan culture," Susan explained. "But they don't have advanced degrees. In the museum world, that makes them persona non grata."

She saw the blank looks on the girls' faces. "That's Latin," she explained. "It means people you don't want to hang around with."

The girls nodded. Now they understood.

"John Riggs's explanation of why he was at the party makes sense," Nancy said, "but we still found

104

cinnabar, ink, and paper in his office. Things aren't looking good for him."

"Is there any evidence that would put him at the scene of the crime?" Susan asked.

"Nothing substantial," Nancy told her. "Briscoe says Riggs wasn't seen at Beech Hill in any of the days leading up to the theft."

"We have to look elsewhere then," Susan declared. "I just can't see Riggs as a thief."

"I do have other leads," Nancy replied. "Henrik van der Hune said he had the provenance documents with him that morning for a reason that he can't remember. But he says they hold a clue."

"They must," Susan agreed. "Especially since Martinez seemed to want them so badly."

"Can I see them again?" Nancy asked.

"Sure," the director replied. "I took them out of my drawer and put them back in Henrik's office. Let's go get them."

The three girls followed her out her door, down the hall, and into Henrik van der Hune's office.

"I put them in his side drawer," Susan said, pulling the drawer open. "That's funny." She groped around inside. "They're not here." Her face froze.

"Are you sure you put them in that drawer?" Nancy asked.

"Positive," Susan said, her voice rising anxiously. "They're gone!"

12

A Slippery Character

Susan Caldwell raced back toward her office. The girls followed her as she poked her head into her assistant's office.

"Sally, has anyone been in Henrik's office today?" she demanded.

Sally shook her head. "Not that I've seen."

"Has anyone borrowed the provenance documents?" Susan asked anxiously. Again Sally shook her head.

"Let's go back to Mr. van der Hune's office and look around more carefully," Nancy suggested. "Maybe they're lying around somewhere else."

The four of them turned the office upside down as they hunted for the documents. But they were nowhere to be found.

"I don't even have any copies," Susan moaned, plopping miserably down in the desk chair. "It usually isn't necessary, since we're such a small museum."

"Doesn't Taylor Sinclair have copies?" Nancy asked.

Susan nodded. "At least there's some available record," she stated. She buried her face in her hands. "When will this end?"

Nancy put a comforting hand on Susan Caldwell's shoulder. "As soon as possible—I promise," she said. "We're going straight to Briscoe's office now for an update. I'll call you later."

Nancy, Bess, and George drove back to the Georgetown police station. When they entered Briscoe's office, he had a computer printout in front of him. He handed it to Nancy. "This list matches the license plate numbers you wrote down with their owners' names," he said. "Take a look."

Nancy wasn't surprised to see John Riggs's name on the list—he'd already admitted he was there. But none of the other names looked familiar. It was no surprise that Ricardo Martinez's name hadn't shown up.

Quickly, she brought Briscoe up to date on the latest development: the disappearance of the provenance documents.

"I only saw Taylor Sinclair's copies the morning after the crime," said Briscoe.

"Van der Hune had the originals with him that morning," Nancy said. "But then he was hurt."

"So Taylor Sinclair's the only one with copies?" Briscoe asked.

Nancy nodded.

Briscoe seemed lost in thought for a moment. Then he remembered something. "I've got the results of that cinnabar sample," he said, waving some computer paper. "It matches up. The stuff in the bottle is the same stuff that's on the notes," he said.

"I'm not surprised," Nancy commented.

"I'm bringing John Riggs in for questioning," Briscoe said. "He'll be here later this afternoon. Want to stop by?"

Nancy quickly agreed, flattered that Briscoe wanted to include her. "Sure," she told him.

The girls stopped for lunch at a little café on Wisconsin Avenue, the main thoroughfare that wound through Georgetown. Over thick club sandwiches, they decided to pay a visit to Taylor Sinclair to look at his copies of the provenance documents.

Taylor was finishing lunch when Nancy stepped into his office. Bess and George waited outside in the gallery.

He motioned for her to sit while he brushed crumbs off his desk with a thick damask napkin. He tossed the napkin onto his plate, then handed a silver tray to his assistant, who took it out.

"How are you today?" he asked Nancy, adjusting his silk tie.

"Fine," she replied.

"And how is the investigation?" he asked. "Coming along?"

Something about Taylor Sinclair's personality rubbed Nancy the wrong way. "We're making some progress," she replied curtly.

"Good," he said, acting completely uninterested. "If you don't mind my asking, why are you here?"

"The originals of the provenance documents are gone," she said. "They've disappeared out of Henrik van der Hune's office."

"Hmmm," Taylor commented. "Detective Briscoe and I couldn't find the originals the morning after the theft either."

"Van der Hune had them with him that morning," Nancy said. "But they were returned to his office after he was hurt. Now they've disappeared."

"And you assume someone stole them?" Taylor asked in a bored voice.

Nancy nodded.

He shrugged. "Who would want them? The sale is old business."

"I was hoping you might have some insight into the details of the sale," Nancy told him. "Anything more I can learn may help me with the case."

"The sale of the carving to Beech Hill was completely aboveboard," Sinclair replied. "I'm not sure what might help you. There was nothing mysterious about it."

"I think Ricardo Martinez may be involved in the theft," Nancy said. "Do you know him?"

"Ricardo!" Sinclair exclaimed. "You really think he's involved?" He laughed.

"Yes, I do," Nancy said. "He told Alejandro del Rio that he knows who stole the carving."

Sinclair continued to laugh loudly. "My dear," he said finally, "if I know Ricardo, he has no idea who stole the carving. All he's trying to do is make a bit of money out of this unfortunate occurrence. That's how he operates. He's a complete scoundrel."

"So you don't think he has anything to do with the theft?" Nancy asked.

Sinclair shook his head vehemently. "Ricardo is a small-time crook," he pronounced. "Stealing the carving of Lord Pacal would be out of his league. He's more of an art shoplifter."

While he chuckled at his own joke, Nancy mulled over his words. From what Alejandro had said, Martinez was far from a small-time thief. Was Taylor Sinclair trying to mislead her? Or did he just have a different opinion about what was major-league art in the art world?

Sinclair's intercom buzzed. He picked up the phone, frowned, and asked his assistant to have whoever it was call him back. Then he frowned again. Apparently, the caller would not be put off.

He put his hand over the mouthpiece. "I've got to take this," he said.

"Please do," Nancy said. "I just wanted to ask if I could look at your copies of the provenance documents."

Sinclair looked annoyed. "I have no idea where they are," he said sharply. "You'll have to get back to me on that."

Frustrated, Nancy whirled around and left his office. She could hear him speak smoothly into the phone. "Yes, yes," he murmured. "Next week, I promise."

When she stepped into the gallery, Bess and George were bent over a display of pre-Columbian jewelry. Sinclair's assistant sat at his desk. Nancy glanced at his nameplate: Jim Nelson. The name seemed familiar for some reason.

"Can I help you?" he asked.

Nancy thought fast. "Yes, you can," she replied. "Mr. Sinclair said I could borrow his copies of the provenance documents for the Lord Pacal carving."

Jim nodded and walked over to the file cabinet. He quickly located the file and handed her the copies.

"Thank you, Jim." Nancy smiled politely. "Come on, guys," she called to Bess and George. They hurried after her as she rushed down the stairs.

Out on the sidewalk, George turned to Nancy. "What's up?"

"I got copies of the provenance documents," she

explained. "Let's just hope Sinclair's assistant doesn't mention to his boss that he gave them to me."

"What happened with Sinclair?" asked Bess.

"He clearly wasn't happy to see me," Nancy replied. "And he wasn't about to give me the documents. Something weird is going on with him. I think we should add him to our list of suspects."

Glancing at her watch, Nancy saw that it was time to return to the Georgetown police station to sit in on John Riggs's questioning. "Why don't you two head back to the hotel and wait for me there," she said. "George, hold on to these copies of the provenance documents. I need to take a look at them later."

In Briscoe's office John Riggs was sitting across from the detective. He looked angry. Nancy was surprised he had come alone. Was he so sure of his innocence that he thought he didn't need a lawyer?

"I've been talking to Mr. Riggs here. Maybe you'd like to hear his story, too," Briscoe said to Nancy. His face showed no trace of emotion.

Nancy turned to John Riggs and waited for him to speak.

"Detective Briscoe tells me that the cinnabar sample you took from the jar in my office matches up with the cinnabar found in the notes." He cleared his throat. "Apparently that's enough to arrest and charge me with the theft of the carving of Lord Pacal."

"Possession of incriminating evidence," Detective Briscoe stated.

"That's just it," Riggs said. "I never ordered that cinnabar. And I certainly never brought it into my office."

"How did it get there then?" Nancy asked.

"I think it was planted," Riggs said firmly. He saw the surprise on Nancy's face and continued. "After you left the other day I did a little detecting work of my own."

Nancy glanced at Detective Briscoe. He sat listening carefully.

"I called the chemical house and asked them about the order I supposedly made," Riggs told them. "Well, there was an order in my name. I asked them to what address it had been sent. They told me it went to a post office box number in downtown Washington."

Nancy's eyes returned to Briscoe. He sat there silently.

"I don't have a post office box," John Riggs protested. "I think someone's trying to frame me!"

13

A Clue from the Past

"I checked it out," Briscoe told Nancy as she sat puzzling over John Riggs's announcement. "The chemical house confirmed that the cinnabar was sent to a post office box number." He waved a sheet of paper. "I've got a search warrant. I'm going downtown to learn more about this box. Like to come?"

Nancy nodded. "I'd like to come, too," Riggs spoke up. "My name and reputation are at stake here."

Detective Briscoe shook his head, then abruptly changed his mind. "Okay," he told Riggs.

Nancy was puzzled. Why would Briscoe allow a suspect to come along on an investigation? Maybe

Briscoe thought Riggs could help them answer any questions that came up—or incriminate himself further.

The three of them hopped into the detective's unmarked sedan. The detective navigated the busy city streets to a small brick post office.

Briscoe flashed his police badge and the search warrant at one of the postal workers behind the counter. They were quickly led into a back office, where Detective Briscoe gave the box number to a short man with a balding head.

The clerk checked his files, then wrote down the name on a sheet of paper and handed it to Briscoe. Briscoe showed it to Riggs. "Look familiar?" he asked.

Riggs shook his head.

Nancy took the paper from Briscoe. "Jim Nelson!" she exclaimed. "He's Taylor Sinclair's assistant. And . . ." Her voiced trailed off as she tried to think of where else she'd seen his name. "He's listed on the printout of car owners at that house last night!"

"Let's go," Briscoe commanded.

Without another word, the two men and Nancy got into the detective's car and headed straight for Taylor Sinclair's gallery.

When they got there, Jim Nelson was sitting at his desk, leafing through a magazine. Briscoe showed him his badge, and the young man sat right up.

"C-c-can I help you?" he stuttered.

"We have a few questions," Nancy told him.

"I'll be happy to answer them," Jim Nelson assured them.

"Do you have a post office box?" Briscoe asked.

The assistant looked puzzled for a second before he responded. "The gallery does," he said. "We were having trouble with our mail delivery here, and Mr. Sinclair decided it might be better to have a post office box. I arranged for it, so it's in my name."

"Did you order a bottle of cinnabar recently and have it sent to that box?" Briscoe asked.

The young man's forehead wrinkled. "Cinnamon?"

"Cinnabar," Briscoe corrected. "It's a red powder."

Jim still looked confused. "No, I didn't," he answered.

Briscoe nodded. "You know I'm looking for the carving of Lord Pacal, don't you?"

"Yes," Jim replied. "And I know you're not having much luck finding it."

"Is that what Taylor Sinclair told you?" Briscoe asked.

Jim Nelson shifted uneasily in his chair. "Yes," he said.

With a glance at Briscoe, Nancy asked, "Do you remember where you were last night?"

Nelson thought for a moment. "I was with some friends at a club in Georgetown until about eleven o'clock," he replied. "Then I went home."

"Your friends will vouch for you?" Nancy asked.

"Of course," Nelson replied.

Briscoe took the printout from his file. "I have a list here of the owners of some cars that were parked by a house in Maryland last night. One of those cars belongs to you." He showed Jim the printout and his name.

Jim put his finger on his name. Nancy saw his hand begin to tremble. He pulled his hand back and put it in his lap. "I was at the club. I swear it," he insisted.

"Did someone else have your car?" Nancy asked.

He was silent.

"Please answer," Briscoe prodded. "I'd like to know, too. Does anyone else drive your car?"

Jim looked down at the desk and let out a deep sigh. "Mr. Sinclair does sometimes," he said, his voice barely above a whisper.

"Did he borrow it last night?" Nancy asked.

"Yes," Jim answered. "He said he'd left his car out at his country place, and he had to go to a meeting in the suburbs."

"Just one more question," she went on. "Who picks up the mail? You?"

Jim shook his head. "No," he said, "the only one who has a key to the box is Taylor Sinclair."

The police detective thanked the assistant and told him he would need to remain available for further questioning. Then Briscoe, Nancy, and Riggs returned to Briscoe's car.

"Well, I guess you're off the hook now," said Briscoe to Riggs, who sat in the backseat.

"Thanks," Riggs mumbled. "I told you I wasn't involved."

Nancy turned around to face Riggs. "What do you make of this?" She told him what she knew about Taylor Sinclair: that he'd argued with Henrik van der Hune at Beech Hill the morning after the theft and that he'd been in the garden just before van der Hune was hurt.

"He's also got money problems," John Riggs added.

This was the first Nancy had heard of this. "Are you sure?"

Riggs nodded. "His sales have been slow this year," he said. "He complained to me about it a couple of months ago."

Nancy and Briscoe looked at each other. This was important information.

"Not many people are aware of it," Riggs went on. "But Taylor Sinclair knows even more about Mayan glyphs than I do. He's also an excellent artist."

"I believe it's time to bring Mr. Sinclair in for questioning," Briscoe announced in a determined tone. "We don't have enough evidence to charge him with anything, but maybe we can get him to reveal something."

"I think you should wait," Nancy spoke up. "During my visit today, I mentioned Ricardo Martinez and the missing provenance documents. Taylor's bound to be at least a little worried. Maybe he'll make some kind of move."

Briscoe considered this. "You may be right, Nancy. But if he is our thief, I don't want him to get away. He could skip the country with that carving."

Nancy nodded. "I know it's a risk," she said. "But I think it's worth it."

"Okay," Briscoe agreed a moment later. "So far you've been right on nearly every count. I'm going to trust your judgment."

"Thank you, Detective," she said, smiling at him. "I'll try not to let you down."

That night Nancy met Bess and George at the hotel restaurant for dinner. Her father had to attend a dinner meeting, but he had promised to meet them later.

"Alejandro called while you were out, Nancy," Bess said, looking up from her menu. "I told him to meet us here so you could fill him in on the latest developments in the case."

"Good," Nancy said. "Luckily, there's a lot to

tell him." She proceeded to bring her friends up to date on the day's events. Bess and George listened wide-eyed when she got to the part about Jim Nelson, the post office box, and his borrowed car.

"So Taylor Sinclair was at the ceremony, too!" George exclaimed. "Do you think Sinclair could have been involved in drugging your hot cocoa?"

"Maybe," said Nancy. "According to John Riggs, he's desperate for money—that's usually a strong motive."

"*Always* a strong motive," a young man's voice said behind them.

Nancy turned around in her seat. "Hi, Alejandro."

The Mexican diplomat pulled out a chair and sat down with the girls. "Tell me your news," he said.

Briefly, Nancy told him what she had just told her friends—that John Riggs had been cleared of any wrongdoing and that Taylor Sinclair was rapidly becoming their prime suspect.

"That still leaves Ricardo Martinez's involvement a big question mark," she finished. "I can't figure out how he fits in."

"It is a puzzle," Alejandro agreed. He pointed to the folder lying on the table. "What's this?"

Nancy picked it up. "These are Taylor Sinclair's copies of the provenance documents," she said. "I hate to admit I've been sneaky, but I managed to trick Jim Nelson into giving them to me."

Alejandro opened the folder. "These are copies of the originals that disappeared?"

Nancy nodded. "When we saw Henrik van der Hune this morning at the hospital, he told us that there was something wrong with the provenance documents," she explained.

"What exactly?" Alejandro asked.

"Unfortunately, he can't remember," Nancy told him. "But I have a feeling that if we could figure out what it is, we'd be able to solve this mystery."

Alejandro flipped through the sheets of paper in the file. "Here's the first bill of sale." He showed it to Nancy.

She held it in her hand. "Yes. The record of the Petersens' buying the carving from the museum in Los Angeles." She looked at the piece of paper thoughtfully. "They live near George's aunt in Connecticut."

She glanced at the address, then felt a prickle of excitement on the back of her neck. "George, didn't you notice the zip code when we looked at the originals?" she asked.

George took the paper. "Yes," she said. "I realized that the Petersens lived in the same town as my aunt."

"But look at this." Nancy thrust the paper at her friend. "Do you see a zip code on Sinclair's copy?"

George shook her head.

"Look at the date," Nancy told her.

"Nineteen fifty-five," George said. She thought about it for a minute. "Hey!" Suddenly she realized what Nancy had noticed.

"There were no zip codes in 1955!" Nancy crowed triumphantly. "I'll bet this bill of sale is a phony!"

14

Ring Around the Robber

"Nancy, what are you saying?" asked Bess.

"That when Taylor Sinclair was trying to sell the statue to Beech Hill, he furnished a phony bill of sale," Nancy explained. "He had to account for the carving's provenance, which he couldn't do without a record."

"In other words, he just made up Lord Pacal's history," Bess said.

"Exactly," Nancy told her friend.

"But he originally made a mistake and put a zip code on the Petersens' address," Alejandro put in.

"Then, realizing his mistake, he altered the copy he showed Briscoe and us so we wouldn't find out," finished George.

"He was probably the one who stole the originals

from Beech Hill, too," Nancy mused. "He didn't want anyone to catch his slipup."

"Perhaps Sinclair also stole the carving to keep anyone from finding out he'd faked the documents," Alejandro pointed out. "The phony bill of sale calls the whole provenance of the carving into question. If the carving never belonged to the Petersens, then where did he get it?"

When Carson Drew joined them in the restaurant a few minutes later, Nancy told him about their discovery. He agreed that the original document had to be a phony. "But you'll need proof," he reminded them. "The original is gone."

"That is a problem," Nancy agreed. "But one person can help us—Henrik van der Hune. *If* his memory is any better."

Early the next morning, Nancy, Bess, George, and Alejandro arrived at the hospital to find Henrik van der Hune sitting up in bed. He looked much more alert than the last time they'd seen him. He immediately recognized Nancy.

"Ah, the young lady who's looking for Lord Pacal," he said. "I was going to call you as soon as I finished breakfast." He pushed the tray away from his bed and motioned for her to sit.

"Is your memory back?" Nancy asked hopefully.

Henrik nodded. "It seems to be—at least partly. Something came to me when I woke up this morning."

"The bill of sale to the Petersens is a fake, isn't it?" Nancy asked.

"You figured it out!" Henrik declared. He sounded impressed.

Nancy told him how they had come to the discovery just the night before.

"That's what I was arguing about with Sinclair that morning, before I was hurt," Henrik said. "I was the one who approved the purchase of the carving of Lord Pacal, but afterward I felt uneasy about it. Something about that purchase letter of the Petersens didn't sit right with me." He shook his head. "I realized I had made a horrible mistake."

"Was it the zip code that tipped you off?" George asked.

Henrik nodded. "Exactly. I asked Taylor Sinclair about it. Several days before the theft I told him there was something wrong with that letter. At first he seemed very concerned. He suggested the Petersens might have created a phony document to conceal the fact that the piece had been smuggled out of Mexico years ago. He said he would talk to the lawyers representing the Petersens' estate and demand an explanation. Then he would get back to me."

"Did he?" Nancy asked.

"No," he said. "Of course, when the carving disappeared, I was immediately suspicious. Only Susan and I had keys to the storeroom, but I knew

125

Sinclair had been in there several times. I thought he might have figured out how to get in."

"But you didn't mention any of this to the police." Alejandro looked puzzled. "Why not?"

"I wanted to be sure," he replied. "So the next morning I did some investigating. I went to the Mexican consulate. They have a copy of a limited edition catalog of the Petersens' collection, published back in the sixties."

Alejandro nodded.

"You checked to see if the carving of Lord Pacal was in the book?" Nancy asked.

"Right," Henrik van der Hune said. "It wasn't. There was a carving, assumed to be of Lord Pacal, but of very inferior quality."

"And so it had to be Sinclair who faked the document," Nancy said with rising excitement.

"That's what I was accusing him of that morning when you saw us," Henrik replied. "I told him I had the documents to prove it, right in my hand."

"The provenance file," Nancy filled in.

"Yes," Henrik said. "And you know what happened next." He touched his head and winced.

"He pushed over the statue to knock you out so he could steal the documents," said George.

"But I picked them up," Nancy remembered. "I had them in my hand when we brought you out to the ambulance. Sinclair must have been really angry when he ran around that wall and couldn't find them."

126

"Do you know how Ricardo Martinez might fit into all of this?" Nancy asked Henrik.

He shrugged. "Maybe Sinclair was going to sell the carving to Martinez for a huge amount of cash and then disappear from Washington. Martinez has the kind of connections you'd need to sell a piece like the carving."

Nancy nodded. "That's my theory, too."

A few minutes later, the girls and Alejandro said goodbye to Henrik and headed once again for Taylor Sinclair's gallery. As they parked outside, Nancy drew a deep breath. She wondered how she was going to force a confession from Sinclair without the faked documents in hand.

Jim Nelson was sitting at his desk.

"Mr. Sinclair isn't here," he said as soon as he saw them. "He's gone to his house in the country."

"Can you give me the address?" Nancy asked.

Jim avoided her eyes. "I've been told not to give out that information," he said.

Nancy gulped. She'd practically promised Detective Briscoe that Sinclair wouldn't get away. What if they couldn't find him?

"You know you'd be an accessory to a crime if what we think about Taylor Sinclair is true," Nancy stated.

"What exactly is he suspected of?" Jim asked uneasily.

"Of stealing the carving of Lord Pacal from Beech Hill," Nancy said. "We think Taylor got it on the black market and phonied up documents for it."

Jim's face turned pale.

"Now will you tell us where his country house is?" Nancy asked.

"I'll write down the address for you," he agreed. His tone turned bitter. "I don't know why I should feel any loyalty toward the man. I haven't been paid in weeks."

"Mr. Sinclair's been having money problems, hasn't he?" Nancy asked.

Jim nodded. "The past year hasn't been a good one."

He stood up to find the address, and Nancy paced the gallery as she waited. In front of a display case she paused to look at the objects inside: a strange carving in the shape of a jaguar, several hammered gold pieces of monkeys and snakes. And then her eyes lighted on a gold and jade ring—a ring she'd seen before.

"Bess, George, Alejandro! Come here!" Nancy pointed to the ring. "I saw this ring the night of the ceremony!"

"What?" Bess rushed over.

"The man who handed me the drink was wearing it!" Nancy exclaimed.

"That must have been Taylor Sinclair," George declared.

"He probably put the sedative in the cup before he handed it to you," Bess added.

128

"Here's the address," Jim Nelson called out. He handed Nancy a piece of paper with a Virginia address on it.

Nancy took it from him. "If you call and tell him we're coming, you'll be aiding and abetting an alleged criminal," she warned.

The assistant nodded. "I'm going to leave the gallery," he declared. "I think Taylor's taken advantage of me long enough."

As Nancy and her friends were about to descend the stairs to the street, the door below opened. A man entered the hallway.

"Martinez!" Alejandro called out. He dashed down the stairs.

Ricardo Martinez immediately turned and bolted out the door.

Nancy followed Alejandro down the stairs. "Someone call Briscoe!" she shouted.

"I'll do it," Bess replied.

When Nancy reached the street, her eyes darted in every direction to see which way Martinez had gone. Finally she spotted him, running down the sidewalk to their right.

"There he is!" She pointed him out, and they sprinted after him.

Martinez was fast on his feet. They chased after him for several blocks, then he darted down a narrow alley.

It's a dead end, Nancy realized, elated. He has nowhere to go.

Martinez let out several Spanish curses. Then he whirled around to face them. "I am warning you. Do not come closer," he shouted.

As Martinez tried to leap around them, George lunged forward and grabbed the tail of his jacket. He quickly shrugged off the coat and ran.

Nancy threw herself at him, knocking him to the ground. She quickly managed to pin him to the sidewalk. George and Alejandro rushed over to help.

As Martinez's eyes met hers, she glowered at him and said, "Now, Mr. Martinez, you're going to tell us everything you know about the theft of Lord Pacal."

15

A Last-Minute Confession

As Nancy held Martinez to the ground, he refused to speak. He just shook his head back and forth. A few minutes later Bess trotted up. "I called Briscoe. He said he'd be at the gallery any minute," she reported. "I'll wait there and let him know where you are."

It didn't take long for Detective Briscoe to arrive in the alley. The officers yanked Martinez to his feet and led him to the van. Nancy and her friends followed the police van to the station.

When Nancy entered the interrogation room, Martinez sat in a wooden chair while Briscoe stood, pacing around the room.

"You know you've been implicated in the theft of the Lord Pacal carving, don't you?" Briscoe asked.

Martinez nodded.

"Anything you say here can be used against you in court," Briscoe warned him.

Martinez shrugged. "I said I don't want a lawyer," he said. "I don't trust them."

"I've read you your rights—you know you're entitled to have one here, right?"

Martinez shook his head. "I said I don't want one," he repeated.

"Okay. Let's start at the beginning," Briscoe said. "Tell us who stole Lord Pacal from Beech Hill."

"I don't know," Martinez said.

Briscoe gave him a skeptical look.

"I don't," Martinez declared. "I swear."

"Do you know how the carving found its way to the United States?" asked Briscoe.

Martinez shifted in his chair.

"Come on," Briscoe chided him. "You and I both know what you do for a living."

Martinez gave him a dirty look.

"I can tell you right now, if you cooperate, we'll go easier on you," Briscoe pointed out. "There's no doubt in my mind you'll do some jail time, but how much time is up to you."

Martinez was silent for a moment, thinking about that. "You've got nothing on me," he said defiantly.

"We've got assault," Briscoe corrected him. "You attacked Ms. Drew here at the Tidal Basin and nearly attacked her again that night out in Maryland. And we have reason to believe you're involved in the Lord Pacal theft." He paused for a moment. "You can bet that when we bring in Taylor Sinclair, he'll point the finger at you. So why not make it easy on yourself and tell us the truth now?"

Briscoe's last remark seemed to work. "I found it," Martinez finally said. "I found the carving of Lord Pacal in Mexico sometime last year."

Nancy leaned forward in her chair.

"A peasant brought it to me," Martinez went on. "The guy said he saw it on a table of junk at a marketplace near the ruins of Palenque. It looked interesting and very old. I knew it was worth something, so I mentioned it to someone who would know for sure."

"Taylor Sinclair?" Briscoe asked.

Martinez nodded. "I brought it into the country and showed it to him," he said.

"You mean you smuggled it into the country," Briscoe added.

Martinez didn't comment on that. "Sinclair got very excited when he saw it," he recalled. "He said he could get millions for it. And he'd share the money with me." Martinez laughed. "I believed him."

"Then Sinclair made some phony documents," Briscoe prompted, "and tied it all into the stuff the Petersens' lawyers were selling."

"I guess so," Martinez said. "All I know is that he offered it to a couple of museums and collections.

After he sold it to Beech Hill, I asked him for my cut. He kept saying I'd get it soon."

Nancy cleared her throat. "Sinclair is having money troubles," she said. "His assistant hasn't been paid in weeks."

Martinez gave a cynical laugh. "Well, at least I'm not alone."

"So what did you do when Sinclair didn't pay up?" Briscoe asked.

"Before I could do anything," Martinez explained, "the carving was stolen."

"Did Sinclair steal it?" asked Briscoe.

"I don't know." Martinez shrugged. "Sinclair told me John Riggs stole it."

Briscoe looked surprised.

"Sinclair said Riggs was jealous," Martinez went on. "He wanted it for his museum. Then Sinclair said if I ever wanted to see my money, I'd have to do a little more work—telling certain people that John Riggs stole the carving."

"Like Alejandro del Rio?" asked Nancy.

He nodded.

So that's why Martinez was trying so desperately to get in touch with Alejandro, Nancy realized.

"And that phone call to me in the middle of the night," Nancy added. "That was you, too?"

Martinez nodded. "He told me I had to get those documents in the file away from you," he said. "That's why I tried to grab them at the Tidal Basin."

"I knew you were after them," Nancy said. "And then you burglarized my hotel room."

Martinez immediately looked surprised. "No, I didn't do that," he protested. "I don't know anything about that."

Nancy was surprised. If Martinez wasn't the intruder, who was? So far, Sinclair had carefully avoided getting his hands dirty; it didn't seem likely he'd risk breaking into a hotel room.

"Tell us about that night at the house in Maryland," she asked, curious.

"I was supposed to meet del Rio to tell him face-to-face the stuff Sinclair told me to say about John Riggs," Martinez explained. "Then I saw Sinclair putting you into the shed. I argued with him—I told him he was going too far. But he told me if I wanted my money, I would have to put you out of the detective business permanently."

"Which you tried to do," Nancy reminded him.

"I didn't want to, I swear it!" Martinez shook his head. "I was glad when del Rio stopped me."

"Was it you who planted the cinnabar and ink and brushes in Riggs's office?" Nancy asked.

"Sinclair made me do that," he admitted.

"Sinclair wrote the notes," Nancy murmured to Briscoe. "He must have stolen the carving, too."

Briscoe nodded. "Now, if we can just find Sinclair with the carving on him, we've got him."

Nancy pulled out from her pocket the slip of paper with Sinclair's country address on it. "He's in

135

Virginia," she said. "I've got the address. Why don't I drop in on him?"

"Okay," Briscoe said. "Meanwhile, I'll get a warrant and search the gallery in case he hid the carving there."

Several police officers led Martinez away, and Briscoe found a Virginia map for Nancy and gave her a special phone number for reaching him. Then Nancy, Bess, George, and Alejandro sped off to Virginia.

Forty minutes later they were winding along a country road. Following the map, they turned onto a dirt lane lined with trees. The road came out to a charming bungalow, perched on a low bluff above the Potomac. There was no sign of a car anywhere.

"It looks like we missed him," Alejandro said worriedly as they all got out of the car.

"Why don't you and Bess check the grounds," Nancy suggested. "George and I will try inside."

As Bess and Alejandro darted around the side of the house, Nancy and George walked to the front door. Nancy was about to knock when she noticed the door was open. "Hello?" she called, pushing it all the way open. "Anyone home?"

She stepped into the front hallway. On one side was a dining room, on the other, a small living room decorated in English chintz and expensive antiques.

"It looks like Sinclair took off," George said.

Nancy nodded.

"I guess so," she said, swallowing her disappointment. "The problem is, I don't have the faintest idea where he might go. Unless Bess and Alejandro found him outside."

She was about to leave the house when she heard a humming noise coming from the dining room. A laptop computer sat on the dining room table. Its screen had dimmed, but it was still on and running.

"Look." She pointed out the computer to George. "He must have left in a hurry. I wonder what he was doing on the computer?"

Nancy went over to the computer and struck a key. The screen flickered on.

Numbers and letters arranged in columns filled the screen. What did they mean? Nancy wondered.

Then suddenly she noticed a set of initials: DCA. She'd seen those same initials on a tag on her suitcase when she'd claimed her luggage at National Airport. "He was checking out flight schedules!" she exclaimed.

"What?" George joined her by the computer. The cursor flashed under the initials DCA. Opposite them was another set of initials: LGA.

"What airport uses the initials LGA?" Nancy asked.

"LaGuardia," George said promptly. "In New York."

"There's no car here!" Nancy reasoned. "I'm betting that Sinclair is on his way to the airport."

She quickly consulted her watch. "How long do you think it will take us to get to National Airport?" she asked, already moving toward the door.

"I'll bet half an hour," said George.

"You'd better be right," Nancy said as they hurried outside. "Because his flight leaves in forty-five minutes. That's barely enough time to find him."

Alejandro and Bess quickly confirmed that there was no sign of Sinclair outside. Nancy jumped in the car and started it up. Alejandro directed her to the airport, which was located in the Virginia suburbs across the river from Washington, D.C.

Thirty minutes later they pulled up to the main terminal at National Airport. The car's brakes squealed as Nancy barreled into a parking spot and stopped the car.

The four of them ran into the terminal. Sinclair's flight was on the Skyair shuttle, boarding at Gate 16. An overhead sign pointed them to the right.

They dashed down a corridor lined with shops, then raced down an escalator. Luckily, there was no line at the security check. They quickly passed through the security scanners and ran for Gate 16, at the end of the hall.

As Nancy ran, she yelled to George to call Detective Briscoe on his special number and get him to the airport right away.

Nancy reached the gate just as the boarding clerk handed Taylor Sinclair his ticket.

"Stop!" Nancy called. "Stop that man!"

The startled attendant looked up. Taylor Sinclair ignored Nancy's cry and calmly stepped toward the jetway.

"You must believe me," Nancy gasped to the clerk. "That man is transporting stolen goods."

"I'm sorry." The clerk held up his hands helplessly.

"Please," Alejandro added, rushing over to the desk. "She's telling the truth. That man must be stopped."

"The police will be here any moment," Nancy went on. "But they may not make it before that plane takes off. Can't you do something?"

Reluctantly, the clerk turned and entered the jetway. He returned a moment later with Taylor Sinclair following behind him.

"How charming," Taylor purred when he saw Nancy. "You've come to see me off."

"I've come to accuse you of stealing the carving of Lord Pacal," Nancy corrected him.

"Ah," Sinclair said. "You must have been talking to that delightful art thief Martinez."

"That's right," Nancy said. "He told us how he smuggled the carving for you."

Sinclair smiled. "That's a good one." He noticed Alejandro. "Helping Ms. Drew play detective, I see."

"Give it up, Taylor," Alejandro told him. "It's all over. The police know everything."

139

Nancy pointed to the carry-on bag Sinclair was holding. "Is that all you're taking?"

"I'm just going to New York overnight to visit a client," Sinclair replied. "Would you like to search my luggage?"

"Actually, I would." She took the bag, placed it on the counter, and went through its contents. She wasn't surprised when she didn't find anything. Maybe he had checked some luggage as well and wasn't mentioning that.

She handed the bag back to him. "I know you stole the carving," Nancy told him. "All the clues point to you."

"And where's your proof?" he asked her, a smirk flitting across his face.

Nancy knew he had her there. Without the original provenance documents or the jade in his possession or his fingerprints on any of the evidence, she had no proof.

"You can't prove it, and you know it," Sinclair said. He picked up his bag off the counter. "I'll see you when I get back from New York," he said. "We'll have lunch. And chat."

He began to board the plane.

As she watched him go, Nancy felt so frustrated —she knew he was guilty, but there was no way to prove it. Wearing jeans and cowboy boots Taylor Sinclair walked away casually as if he were an ordinary tourist about to spend a few days in New York.

Then it dawned on her. Cowboy boots—what an odd choice for Sinclair. She'd never seen him in anything less formal than well-polished black tassel loafers.

Oh my gosh, she thought. What better place to hide something small than the large heel of a cowboy boot!

16

Many Happy Returns

"Stop that man!" Nancy cried again to the airline clerk. "He *does* have stolen goods on him—and now I know where!"

This time, when Sinclair heard Nancy's cries, he panicked. He wheeled around and bolted toward the right of the terminal.

Nancy took off after him. As he raced up the terminal hallway, Sinclair shoved people aside.

Suddenly he slipped through a tiny aisle beyond the security check. Nancy was right behind him.

The aisle led to another wide corridor. Taylor Sinclair flung himself onto an escalator, taking the moving steps two at a time. Nancy charged up the stairs directly to the right. She could hear Alejandro running right behind her.

142

When Sinclair reached the top of the escalator, she threw herself at him. He toppled over in front of a newsstand.

Alejandro quickly pinned Sinclair's arms to the floor. "Take off your boots," Nancy ordered Sinclair.

"That's a little unnecessary, isn't it?" he said, twisting his head around to look up at Nancy.

"If you won't take them off, I will," Alejandro threatened him.

"Then kindly let go of my arms," Taylor said.

Alejandro let go but stayed close in case Sinclair decided to bolt again. By this time, Bess and George had caught up to them, too, and hovered nearby.

Wordlessly, Sinclair removed his boots and set them on the floor. Nancy reached for them and twisted one heel. Nothing. The heel stayed on.

She looked at Sinclair. For the first time, his face registered emotion, and the emotion was fear. I'm on the right track, Nancy thought.

She picked up the other boot and twisted its heel. Immediately, it came off in her hand.

Something fell into her palm—a greenstone carving. She turned it over. The face of Lord Pacal looked back at her. After looking so often at the photo of the carving, she was amazed to see how tiny the real thing was and how perfectly cut. No wonder it was so valuable and so many people had wanted it.

"I've found it!" she exclaimed. She showed the carving to her friends.

Sinclair groaned.

Then they heard pounding feet. They looked up to see Detective Briscoe turning a corner as he hurried toward them.

"You got him!" Briscoe exclaimed as he saw Sinclair sitting despondently on the floor. "Good work, young lady!"

He approached Sinclair. "You're under arrest," he informed him. "And you're going to tell us everything when we get back to the station."

Taylor Sinclair slumped in a chair next to Briscoe's desk.

"Ask away," he said with a wave of his hand.

Nancy hardly knew where to start. She looked at Detective Briscoe.

"You solved it," he said. "You ask the questions."

Nancy turned to Sinclair. "We already know how Martinez found the carving and passed it on to you," she began. "We know you faked the documents to make the piece look genuine and later changed your copies to cover up the mistake with the zip code. Where are the originals?"

"I sent them up to New York," Sinclair said. "They're with a friend."

"Write down the address," Briscoe ordered. "We'll have someone up there get them."

Sinclair wrote down the address and handed the slip of paper to Briscoe.

"You burglarized my room looking for them, didn't you?" Nancy asked.

Sinclair nodded. "On the off chance that you'd figure out their importance," he murmured, giving her a scathing look. "I managed to persuade a chambermaid to let me in."

Nancy ignored his put-down. "And it was you who wrote those death threats, too, wasn't it?" she accused him.

"Obviously, they didn't have the effect I was hoping for," he murmured.

"You wanted to scare me off," Nancy said. "I don't scare easily."

"I can see that," Sinclair remarked drily. "When van der Hune found me out, I realized I had to get that carving out of Beech Hill as soon as possible. Luckily, I knew just where they kept it, and I managed to sneak away Henrik van der Hune's keys and copy them. Such an innocent—he never knew. And no one even questioned why I was down in the storeroom, because I'd been there so often in the past month." Sinclair snapped his fingers. "It was that simple."

"And you framed John Riggs," Nancy continued. "You ordered the cinnabar in his name and planted the materials for making the notes in his office."

He stared at her silently.

"Then you used Martinez to spread rumors that Riggs stole the carving," she added. "But what did you intend to do with the carving after you stole it?"

"Resell it," Sinclair said. "There are lots of people with money who don't care about an object's provenance as long as they like it."

"And you needed the money," Nancy reminded him. "Your gallery is in trouble."

Sinclair looked surprised. "How did you know that?" he asked.

"You made the mistake of telling John Riggs a while ago," Nancy told him. "And you haven't paid your assistant in weeks."

He sighed. "What does it matter? It's all over now, isn't it?"

"I'm afraid it is," Detective Briscoe chimed in. "I've got some people waiting now who'd like to take your fingerprints."

"Just one more question," Nancy said. There was something nagging at her. "Why did you drug me that night at the ceremony? It was you, wasn't it?"

"You were getting too close," Sinclair replied. "Asking too many questions. When I spotted you at the party, I decided to try to get you out of the way. I found some prescription sedatives in our hostess's medicine chest. Everything went fine—until Alejandro del Rio came to your rescue."

At that, Taylor Sinclair shrugged and stood up.

146

He let Briscoe lead him out to the booking room. It's all over, thought Nancy. The mystery is solved. But one last question remained—what to do with the Lord Pacal carving now that it had been found.

It was a glorious spring morning at Beech Hill. The sun was bright in a deep blue sky as a crowd of impatient reporters gathered in the garden for a press conference that Susan Caldwell had called only hours earlier.

On a side terrace Nancy, Carson Drew, Bess, and George stood with Susan Caldwell and Alejandro del Rio, waiting for the event to start.

"Well, Alejandro," Susan said with a smile, "you got your wish. Lord Pacal is going back to Mexico. Now that we know how he came into the country, there's no way we can keep him."

Alejandro gave her a wide smile. "My people will be happy to have their king back," he said with a gracious little bow.

When Susan Caldwell had heard the whole story, her response was swift and sure. She believed Lord Pacal had to go back to Mexico, where he belonged. And Alejandro would be the one to carry him back.

The press conference was a way to let the world know that the newly found king was being returned to his home. Nancy was thrilled to see such an amazing turnout for his sendoff.

Nancy felt a soft tug at her elbow. She turned to

find Alejandro facing her with a small jewelry box in his hand.

"Please accept this as a token of gratitude from my people and from me for all you've done to find Lord Pacal," he said.

Nancy didn't know what to say.

"Open it," Alejandro urged.

Nancy opened the lid. Inside was a greenstone pendant on a gold chain. Mayan glyphs were carved into the pendant. She looked up at Alejandro. "What does it say?"

"The glyphs spell out your name," he said, smiling. "It's not a Mayan name, of course, so I had the carver use glyphs that represent the sounds of each letter of your name."

He pointed to one of the characters. "See this one, that looks like a fish? That's the symbol for the letter *C*." He picked the carving up and placed it into her hand. "Isn't it interesting how *C* in our language looks like something from the sea in yours?" He grinned. "A Mayan pun."

Nancy laughed softly. "I will always treasure this, Alejandro," she said. "Thank you."

"And thank you," he replied. Then, squaring his shoulders, he headed out to the bright lights of the cameras that awaited him and Susan Caldwell.

Nancy fastened the pendant around her neck. The greenstone felt smooth and cool against her skin. Bess and George leaned over to get a look and began to ooh and aah.

"Sssh, girls," Carson Drew said. "The press conference is about to begin."

But not before Bess had her say. She nudged Nancy. "Now," she whispered with a chuckle, "can we finally go to the top of the Washington Monument?"

THE HARDY BOYS® SERIES By Franklin W. Dixon

LOOK FOR
AN EXCITING NEW
HARDY BOYS MYSTERY
COMING FROM
MINSTREL® BOOKS
EVERY OTHER

NANCY DREW® MYSTERY STORIES By Carolyn Keene